Lock Down Publications and Ca$h
Presents

IMMA DIE BOUT MINE

3

Apex Predators Only

By
Aryanna

First Edition 2024

Printed in the United States of America

Lock Down Publications
P.O. Box 944
Stockbridge, GA 30281
www.lockdownpublications.com

Like our page on Facebook: Lock Down Publications
www.facebook.com/lockdownpublications.ldp

Stay Connected with Us!

Text **LOCKDOWN** to 22828 to stay up-to-date with new releases, sneak peaks, contests and more…

Like our page on Facebook:
Lock Down Publications

Join Lock Down Publications/The New Era Reading Group

Visit our website:
www.lockdownpublications.com

Follow us on Instagram:
Lock Down Publications

Email Us: We want to hear from you!

Dedication

This book is dedicated to McKenzie Rain, aka BIG RAIN! I love you because you're beautiful inside and out. Never forget!

Acknowledgements

As always, I thank God first because without him, I'm nothing. I want to thank my family, especially those who ain't blood related because that means you chose to ride this ride with me. That's love. I want to thank my friends, and that's important because that's probably not a label I would've used a few years ago due to my trust issues. I still keep my circle smaller than a period, but I got some real muthafuckas with real love and loyalty for me. I appreciate it.

To my children... I thank you for the struggle because the battles that we have bring me humility and wisdom. We may never agree on everything, but we can talk about anything. Aryanna, I love you no matter where you are or what you do. Lia, you're part of my soul, just like your mother will always be, and I love you. Mariah Grace, what can I say except that I love uuuuuuu! Lol! Jada Boo, you ALREADY KNOW that you're my baby for life! Queen Cade, ayo, I love uuuuuuu, and u know why! Lmao!

To my fans, I promise you love and loyalty like you give me and to keep trying to push out the best product for you. My pen bleeds for you. To my real niggas, shit, we all we got! To my honey, Tabitha Nicole, hold your head, queen, because that crown is heavy. I'll see you in a minute, limo tint included. Lol! I love you, bae! FREE DA FUCKIN MOB!!!! LDP, THE GAME IS OURS!

Chapter 1

(Royal)

Putting my feet back on U.S. soil was something that I swore I'd never do years ago, but from the moment I'd met Tesha, I knew that I'd show up for her. It wasn't like I was wanted by the law out here because I'd gotten that part figured out a while ago. I knew there was still a sour taste in a lot of mouths though about the fact that the Walker family had gotten away with murder. Literally.

My decision about not being in America was because I understood the blood that its government had on its hands. I understood it in an intimate way, and I wanted no parts of the hypocrisy that was the American dream. It was a different kind of dream though that had me go against my word and currently speed walking down the hallway of a hospital in Orlando, Florida. The dream of a life together with Tesha had gotten me this far, but the nightmare was what I stepped into when I finally made it to her room. By nature, I didn't do hospitals but not because I was afraid of death. Death was one of life's certainties, and it was a merciful thing for someone with eyes as experienced as mine. In eighteen years, I'd lived at least as many lifetimes and witnessed all the fuck shit that came with the show. To me, hospitals were purgatory, that in between place between what was and what would never be again. It was a place worse than death because it was the uncertain land of waiting. I needed this hospital in this moment to be different though, and I needed the miracle of life to be breathed back into Tesha. We'd only just found each other so losing her already would be a cruel demonstration of the devil's work.

As I approached the bed where she lay, I thought I could hear the devil's cackle of laughter in the distance, but the slow rise and fall of her chest told me that hell hadn't come to Earth yet. I visually took in the battered condition of her body, the cuts and bruises sporting fresh bandages stained crimson with her blood, and I felt my rage tip the scales at homicidal. The girl that was so full of life, the girl that I'd been falling for, was laid before me, helpless and vulnerable, and somebody would pay for that. They would pay in blood, just like she had, or I wasn't my daddy's son.

"Who-Who are you?" a woman asked, coming out of the bathroom and pulling up short in obvious surprise.

One look at her and the familial resemblance to Tesha and Tynesha was impossible to deny, and that meant that this was their mother.

"My name is Royal."

"Oh, you're the one who called the ambulance to the scene of the accident? The one who called me?" she asked, wiping the tears from her face.

"Yeah, that was me. I was on the phone with Tesha when..."

My voice trailed off because the word accident didn't accurately describe what had happened in and around the car. I knew a hit job when I saw one, but all I'd needed was my ears in this case because I'd heard everything that went down. I'd heard it all. After that, the only thing that I could think to do was hack Tesha's location through her phone and send help. The woman in front of me stepped forward and wrapped her small frame around my 6'4, two hundred twenty pounds and hugged me tight like no one had done since my own mother. Instantly, I felt the lump form in my throat, but I swallowed around it and maintained my composure.

7

"Thank you, Royal. Thank you so much. Your actions saved my daughter and my grandchild, so I can never thank you enough for that."

"You don't have to thank me. It was the least I could do. I only wish that I could've been there to do more," I replied genuinely.

She let me go and took a step back so that she could look up at me.

"If you wanna do more then tell me what really happened, Royal. I know there was a car accident, but that don't explain the two bullets they pulled out of my baby's back. It don't explain where Tynesha is either, and I need those answers. A mother deserves to know."

Her impassioned plea hurt my heart, but I still dreaded giving her the ugliness of truth that would only lead to tragedy. I knew what it was like to need that truth though because, sometimes, you had to break something in order to be made whole and heal properly. My eyes went to the hospital bed where Tesha lay, still effortlessly beautiful in her tranquil sedation. Still helpless. Still vulnerable. But still alive and she would only be made whole again if her twin's life could be saved before it was too late. That knowledge made my decision for me.

"I was talking to Tesha from the plane, excited about finally meeting her in person. She introduced me to Tynesha, and then shit went bad. When the other vehicle hit them, Tesha's phone flew out of her hands and landed on the dashboard, but it didn't disconnect us. I could only see the sky through the window, but I could hear everything."

"They brought her phone in with her, but it wasn't on. It's in her bag over there. What did you hear?" she asked, still wiping tears from her face.

"Tesha must've been unconscious immediately because I never heard her speak again. I heard Tynesha though. She was trying to get Tesha to wake up, and then she called someone named David for help. After that, I heard two gunshots, and then someone told Tynesha to get out of the car or die."

"So, Ty was-was kidnapped by whoever caused the accident? I know that you couldn't see the person's face, but is there anything you can tell me that might help find her?" she asked desperately.

"I'm not sure. I thought that I heard Tynesha say the name Roland though."

The look on her face immediately shifted from that of a grieving, fractured mother to one of horrible understanding. I didn't know who this Roland character was, but he was obviously dangerous, and if he did this, the nigga definitely needed killing.

"You look like you need to have a seat," I recommended, stepping forward and helping her into the chair beside Tesha's bed.

"Th-Thank you, Royal. I'm okay. I'm just pregnant."

"Yeah, Tesha told me," I replied.

It was obvious by the way that she looked up at me that what I'd said had surprised her.

"You and my daughter must be close if she told you something so personal about me or herself. How come I don't know anything about you?"

"Because Tesha wanted to wait until shit calmed down before we all got together. She didn't tell me exactly what the problems were, and I didn't wanna push, but shit is different now, so I need you to tell me what happened. Who's Roland, and why would he do this to your family?" I asked, fighting for calm to remain within for whatever truth I was about to hear.

"It's a long story."

I pulled up a chair right next to hers and sat down so that we were facing each other.

"Tell me," I demanded gently.

After a couple deep breaths, she opened her mouth and began to explain the events of the past several months. Tesha and I had open and honest conversations, but as I listened to her mother speak, I knew why she'd kept all of this from me. If she had told me, she knew I would've come to town sooner, and I would've brought death's warm welcome with me. When Tonya was done talking, I looked over at Tesha lying in bed again, and in my heart, I knew that I'd just inherited whatever beef she had. For her, I wanted ALL the goddamn smoke! I wouldn't involve my family because this was my decision as a man in a showing of loyalty to his woman. It was in my blood to protect what I loved, and I'd admitted to myself not so long ago that I was falling hard for the beautiful unconscious woman before me. No one could fuck with her or her family and get away with it, not as long as I was breathing.

"I'm not gonna let anything happen to Tesha, and I need you to trust me with her life right now," I said.

"I don't even know you, so how could I possibly honor that request?"

"Fair enough. I'll tell you exactly who I am," I replied, getting comfortable in my seat.

We talked softly amongst ourselves for the next few hours until Tesha began to stir awake, which signaled that her sedative was wearing off. Her mom hit the call button, but when the nurse didn't immediately respond, she went to find her ass. I stayed put, and when Tesha's mesmerizing hazel green eyes opened, my face was the first thing she saw.

"You-You really came," she said weakly.

"I tried to fly the damn plane myself after what happened."

"Wh-What happened, Royal?"

"You were in a car accident. Do you remember any of that?" I asked gently.

"I remember talking to you... and showing you off to Ty on the phone, but that's it. Where's Ty? Is she hurt? What about her baby?"

Nobody with a heart or empathy liked to give bad news, so most niggas in my position would've passed her questions off to someone else. I cared too much about her to do that though, so I moved my chair closer to her bed and took her hand in mine. Instantly, fear contorted her features, but I kissed the back of her hand and let her draw strength from me.

"Sweetheart, your sister wasn't killed in the accident, but from what I've been able to put together, I think Roland kidnapped her."

"R-Roland is dead. The police said David killed him a couple months ago," she replied, looking confused.

"One of the things I've learned in this life is that if you didn't personally witness somebody die, then don't assume that they're dead. I heard your sister say the name Roland, and then, I heard a man's voice force her to choose between getting out of the car or dying alongside you."

"Oh, God," she moaned, closing her eyes.

"When I heard that, I thought you-I thought I lost you, and I almost lost my mind, baby."

She opened her eyes back up and looked at me with her love for me burning bright through the ocean of tears that she was trapped under. She squeezed my hands, and I put her hand in between both of mine, hoping to give her more strength. I heard the door open behind me, but I didn't turn around because I figured that it was her mom returning with the nurse. The last thing that I expected was to hear the sound of a gun cocking, but it was a sound that was unmistakable, so I knew what it was.

"Get the fuck away from her," a male voice growled.

"D-David, it's okay," Tesha said.

When I glanced over my shoulder, I was looking down the barrel of a pretty Ruger .45, and the eyes of the man holding it said that he'd use it.

"I won't tell you again," David warned.

"'By her side is where I belong so either pull the trigger, nigga, or get that gun out my face. I won't repeat myself," I replied calmly.

"David, chill," Tonya said, appearing over his left shoulder.

He glanced at her, and that was the small window of opportunity I needed to grab my Sig Sauer .45 and level it at his face.

"You wanna dance?" I asked.

Chapter 2

(Tynesha)

Pain. All I knew was I had pain throughout my whole body, and the turbulent ride on the floor of the panel van I was trapped in only intensified it. I could taste the salt from my tears in my mouth around the gag that prevented me from screaming, and it made me want to vomit. I managed to maneuver my face against the floor of the van to push the gag down, and I was finally able to take a deep breath. The fear that I felt for me and my unborn child made me want to vomit too, but I knew I had to keep it together if I was going to survive this. I didn't know how long we'd been travelling or in what direction, but the clean getaway from a bold daytime abduction told me that Roland had meticulously planned this shit. His mental calculation had been one of the things that attracted me to him when we'd met, but through his cycle of abuse, I'd learned why that very trait was dangerous. Granted, by making us all believe that he was dead, it had allowed him to plan without us being on guard for the bullshit. Still, I knew that the position I was in and the death of my twin sister were my own fault. Even if the rest of my life was short, I still had to live with that truth. My whole family was at war with the streets and its paid for politicians, which meant I should've been keeping a low profile. I'd felt comfortable living in the safety of an apartment building where no law enforcement or opp could go because we had diplomatic immunity, and that made me reckless. Sloppy.

Predictable even because the ways that me and my twin celebrated our birthday were rooted in tradition that anyone who knew us would know. It hadn't crossed my mind that there could be danger in our outing because I'd assumed that the opps I knew didn't know me. I had no idea how I would pay for that assumption, but it was a safe bet that the pain of losing my sister was just the beginning. There would be more pain. If Roland simply wanted me dead then he could've shot me with the same ruthlessness that he displayed gunning down Tesha, but he hadn't. He'd forced me into the all-white, windowless van that smelled like fertilizer and something foreign to my senses. The odds were good that he planned to torture me, so I would have to think on my feet and look for any opportunity to gain the upper hand. The feeling of the van slowing down signaled to me that I needed to think faster because shit was about to get real. I heard one door open and close after we came to a stop, but other than that, all I could focus on was whether to play dead or not. Showing Roland fear in the past was like showing fear to any blood thirsty predator who could smell it on you. It was dangerous because it made them bolder and more brazen. When I'd done that before, he'd hit me, but most times, I was able to protect myself from the worst of it. Now, I was protecting more than me, and my hands were zip tied together, so my tactics had to be different, even if only to buy some time for David to find me.

I was hoping and praying that my David was back stateside because, in my heart, I felt like God had sent him into my life to save it a long time ago. This was probably the biggest test of my faith thus far, but I believed in David like I did in God. When it was my time to die, I'd take that same belief to the grave, but today couldn't be that day. When the van's back doors suddenly popped open, I was forced to squint as my eyes adjusted to the bright afternoon sunlight. I could taste the humidity on my tongue in a familiar way that sent chills rolling through my body like an electrical current. I didn't have to see past Roland's hulking figure to know that we were way out in the glades. I didn't have to question why we were here either because I'd used the same hollowed grounds for the games of torture that this man I used to love was undoubtedly contemplating.

"Wakey, wakey, my sweet Tynesha."

"Ain't nobody sleep, nigga, and stop trying to sound like a white serial killer because we both know that you ain't that smart," I replied, giving all attitude and impatience.

His face was backlit by the sun, making his features harder to see in detail, but the surprise was easy to read in his eyes. The face was definitely new, but the eyes were familiar pages from an old book. He didn't respond. He simply pulled me from the van roughly and placed me on my feet.

"If you run, I'll shoot you and feed you to the gators. It won't be a kill shot either. It'll just be a wound to bring out all the coldblooded predators that will devour you while you're still alive to feel it."

"Sounds interesting," I replied blandly, faking a yawn to amplify my sarcasm.

I could clearly see the annoyance fighting with the surprise now taking ahold of his face, but he didn't do anything more than push me toward the two-story house in the distance. It crossed my mind to sit down and make his bitch ass carry me, but I knew that I had to play my hand slow and steady. So, I walked while taking in my surroundings along the way. The house was obviously old, but it looked well-kept from the outside. We weren't in the heart of the glades, more so on the outskirts, and I could see untamed wildlife growing up behind the house. There was no sign of another car or another soul, which heightened my anxiety, but I fought to control my emotions because that was the difference between life and death. As I walked up the six steps to the front door, I took several deep breaths and mentally prepared for whatever lay behind the stained oak door. He stepped around me to open the door, which made me chuckle because this nigga really thought he was a gangsta and a gentleman. I walked past him, without glancing his way, into the brightly lit entryway where I took stock of my new cage. The furniture was sparse in the living room, just a couch and love seat that were an ugly shade of gray. The stairs leading upward were right in front of me, and I couldn't see any of what was in the back of the house.

Since I didn't know where my capture wanted me, I stood right inside the door and fixed my face with the best bored expression I could work up.

"It's not much, but it's secluded, so we don't gotta worry about someone stumbling up on us." He closed the door behind us.

"Why you talking like this some type of romantic getaway, nigga? I don't give a fuck about this place because a prison is a prison regardless."

"Look, Tynesha, just chill the fuck out, alright? I'm bout sick of your bullshit already, and you're making me regret rescuing your ungrateful ass!"

"Rescue me?! Did you really just say that you rescued me, you weird ass nigga?!" I asked in disbelief as the feelings of rage surged through my veins like a boost of adrenaline.

"That's exactly what the fuck I did because I could've left you to die with your nigga, David, and what's left of your family. I mean, did you really think that this war would be so lopsided that you muthafuckas could win without bleeding? Did you think Zoe Pound would take the disrespect and the murdering of their people lightly or lying down? Well, I'm sorry to burst your fantasy bubble, sweetheart, but the fight don't never start until you get hit back."

"You already fucking hit back by killing David's aunt and my sister, fuck nigga!" I growled, turning to face him and wishing that my hands weren't still bound in front of me.

"Your self-righteous indignation is cute, even though it's misplaced. General Umar's wife was killed by friendly fire, and I would know because I was part of the welcoming committee in the parking lot that night."

His revelation made my heart stop, but I immediately doubted he was being honest because I knew just how smoothly that this nigga could lie.

"Yeah, whatever. The point is that we didn't start this shit. You did when you wouldn't let me go, you obsessed stalker," I said, growing more frustrated.

"Name calling? That's what you've been reduced to? I see that your time spent locked in that apartment building has forced you into a more primitive form of communication. That's okay though because you'll learn how to be nicer to me, and once you see that safe haven you've been hiding in disappear, you'll realize that you owe me your life."

"Wh-What do you mean disappear? It's almost impossible to knock that building down," I said, fighting against the fear I felt rising like bad blood pressure.

"You're thinking too literal, baby. No one has to knock a building down in order to take away the safety that was provided to all of you. All we had to do was convince the board members that David, and his guests, were liabilities that would only increase the amount of eyes looking in their direction the longer they stayed under their protection. Those men existed comfortably in the shadows long before all of you brought the bullshit to their doorstep. Literally. They value that anonymity more than they fear upsetting General Umar. Umar is but one man with one army, and he's starting to operate on foreign soil in ways that define domestic terrorism. His days are numbered because he's very quickly made himself persona non grata with the United States. Without his protection, those same men who offered you all safety will now devour you just to avoid being eaten. The laws of the jungle are simple. It's all about survival of the fittest."

Everything in my soul wanted to smack smoke from this nigga's mouth, but I didn't because I had to figure out a way to save the people I loved. My stepdaughter, Dayjah, was safe in Africa, but that still left my mom, Shaomi, David, Nyaisha, and Carrie who would be in one of the two apartments. They had no idea that they were now in enemy territory and how I played my hand could affect my ability to warn them.

"The plan seems well thought out, I'll give you that, but what's your end game, Roland? Do you think that saving me while leaving the people that I love to die would somehow make me love you again? Seriously? I mean, I know you ain't the brightest nigga in the world, but this play makes no sense for you, and it sounds like you're getting fucked."

"Oh, yeah? How so?" he asked, looking amused.

"What are you really getting out of this? From the sounds of it, Zoe Pound is the only winner for real, and we both know that you'll never be part of that family. You ain't cut from their cloth. You just do their dry cleaning. So, do the math and tell me how this adds up for you to have anything except a broken heart to go with the swamp grave waiting for you. If WE'RE liabilities, then you have to be able to see that you are too because it was YOU who started all this. You're a dead man who's too dumb to fall down."

I could tell that my words were taking root just like I wanted them to, but I had one more piece to move in order to make the coming checkmate inevitable. I waited a few more seconds without saying anything, just to let his running mind pick up speed, and then I started laughing at him. As predicted, he raised his gun and put it to my forehead.

"You're laughing, but if what you say is true, then I might as well kill you now and vanish," he said, dead serious.

"Go ahead. Kill me and your baby, you silly muthafucka, because I really didn't wanna have a child by your dumb ass anyway."

Chapter 3

(David)

My finger on the trigger was steady despite my heart beat increasing because of his gun being in my face. I didn't focus on the cannon that could permanently shift my thoughts if he chose to pull the trigger. I kept my eyes on him. In his eyes, I saw an unexpected comfort and relaxation, and that was more telling than any words he could've spoken. This nigga was used to the pressures of life and death, and from the looks of it, he was willing to give his life for Tesha. For me, that only created more questions than it answered.

"Who the fuck are you?" I asked.

"That don't matter," he replied nonchalantly.

"It does if you could pose a threat to my family, nigga."

"The only one posing the threat right now is you, and you're also testing my patience. Tesha? Is this who I think it is?" he asked, never taking his brown eyes off of me.

"Yeah, Royal, that's David, my sister's husband."

I could tell that for a split second, this made the nigga want to shoot me more, but in the end, he lowered his gun. It was the smirk that he gave me before he sat back down next to Tesha that almost got his noodle rocked, but I somehow managed to maintain control.

"Ayo, Tesha, who the fuck is this nigga?" I asked, still keeping my gun pointed at the back of his head.

"David, you need to chill the fuck out and stay focused on the bigger problem," Tonya said, moving from behind me until she was standing in front of my gun.

My arm immediately dropped to my side, and the obvious pain in her eyes rekindled the fear that I'd flown into the country with.

"Tell me what happened," I demanded.

As Tonya ran down the details, the feelings of guilt inside me continued to grow until I felt like I was suffocating from them. While my wife was being kidnapped and her sister was shot, I was fucking my ex, Shaomi, who happened to be their cousin. I could've lost two of my kids, and instead of keeping my family safe, I'd been getting my dick wet. I moved to apologize to Tesha, but Tonya side stepped in my way and put her hands on my chest.

"She's okay, and right now, I need you to focus on finding Ty because we know she's still alive, but she's probably hurt too," Tonya said.

"How do we know that?"

"Because if he just wanted her dead then he would've shot her right along with Tesha. As crazy as it sounds, I think Roland still loves Ty, and his plan somehow involves them being together," Tonya replied.

Hearing this made me sick and furious in equal measure, but I was able to control the outrage and focus on harnessing it as motivation. I needed to find my wife as soon as possible.

"Where would he take her?" I asked.

"I have no idea. Can your uncle help?" Tonya asked.

"I don't know. I'm waiting to hear back from him. I expected him to meet me at the airport, but he texted me that he had an unavoidable meeting to attend. I've got his people with me though, and as soon as I know which way to point, them niggas will shoot."

"Can't you track her cellphone or something?" Tonya asked.

"I mean, yeah, I could because..."

"Tynesha don't have her cellphone on her," Royal interjected.

His sudden insertion into the conversation was just the opening I needed, and I wasted no time moving around Tonya to seize it.

"How the fuck do you know what MY WIFE does or doesn't have?" I asked aggressively.

I had positioned myself at the end of Tesha's bed where I could get my shot off before he could grab his gun again.

"I know because I hacked into her phone, along with Tesha's, which was how the rescue squad got there in time. I know because even though Tesha was saved, I still kept looking for Tynesha. I KNOW because I made it my muthafuckin business to know so take that air out of your chest because I'm not that nigga, nigga!"

Everything in me was ready to grease this nigga's scalp with some hot bullets but what Tesha did froze me. She didn't say a word, but she took his hand in hers and forced him to focus on her instead of me. Their silent communication didn't require words to translate it because it was becoming increasingly clear that they were more than friends.

"Tesha, what the fuck are you doing?" I asked, looking at her with growing disgust.

"Whatever she's doing is no longer your concern, not that it ever was, so I suggest you stay focused on finding your wife," Royal said, using a calmer tone that carried more bite than his aggression had.

"You two need to stop this macho, dick swinging contest because it's not helping the situation at all. I need you two to work together to find my sister before it's too late," Tesha pleaded.

"This is a family matter, and we don't need some outside nigga to stick his nose in the business," I replied stubbornly.

"I'm not an outsider to anyone in this room except for you, David, but since you're so curious, I'll introduce myself. I'm Royal Walker, son of FatherGod and heir to the throne of a world that you ain't a part of. I'm the nigga that's gonna take care of the baby that you made with this beautiful queen, your wife's sister, and you should appreciate that. I'm also that nigga who has the resources and skills to be a powerful ally or a brutally formidable opponent. You can choose which you'd prefer."

My eyes locked with Tesha's because the fact that this muthafucka knew that I'd fathered her baby was a betrayal of the trust that I'd thought we had. I couldn't describe how that made me feel, but I knew without a doubt that me being in this room right now was dangerous to everybody.

"I take care of my kids, and I take care of my family. If you get in the way of that, Royal, I'll make sure that your throne is left to the next heir in line," I warned, turning and walking toward the door.

Tonya was smart enough not to say anything, but I heard Tesha calling me as I was tucking my gun into my pants and leaving the room. I didn't so much as glance backwards. I just kept it pushing before I lost the little control that I had left. By the time I got back downstairs to the waiting chauffeured Lincoln Navigator, I was feeling coldblooded and deadly.

"Take me home," I demanded once I was secured behind the truck's mirror tint.

I shot my uncle a text, asking him when he'd be done with his meeting because I needed his help to find Ty. My next move was to reach out to the people I fucked with in the streets to have them find any rock Roland might try to hide under. The police had declared him dead, so it would be a good place to start by finding out which crooked ass cop had passed that notion. Carrie would be able to help me with that, and I knew she was holed up in my apartment with Nyaisha. Fifteen minutes later, I arrived at my apartment building, and I went straight to the twelfth floor where I found both women sitting on the couch, smoking weed.

"What's the word?" Nyaisha asked immediately.

"Tesha's good, Ty's missing, and that hospital room ain't big enough for me and Royal."

"Who's Royal?" Carrie asked.

"Some fuck nigga that's got his head stuck in Tesha's pussy, so he thinks he has an opinion that matters," I replied, still frustrated.

"What? That shit sounds crazy, David. Who is this nigga for real?" Nyaisha asked.

"I told you the nigga said his name was Royal Walker, and he..."

"Wait, did you say Walker?" Carrie asked, passing me the blunt and pulling out her phone.

"Yeah, why?" I asked.

She didn't respond, but her fingers were flying across her phone's screen like a magic trick.

"Do we know where Ty is, or who she wit?" Nyaisha asked.

"Supposedly, her ex-boyfriend, Roland, who we thought was dead, took her at gunpoint," I replied, hitting the blunt.

"Wait, Roland ain't dead? So, how the fuck did you get jammed up with a murder charge for killing him?" Carrie asked, looking up from her phone momentarily.

"That's the part in the movie that I need you to focus on. Find out what cop verified me killing Roland and what information was relied on to confirm that shit. I'mma focus on finding out where this muthafucka is hiding and get my wife back."

"Before we get to that, I need you to read this," Carrie said, passing me her phone and taking the blunt back from my grip.

When I looked at her screen, I saw an old online article written about Jonathan 'FatherGod' Walker and his murderous offspring. As I began to read, there were certain things that jogged my memory because I'd heard about this family a few years ago. It was clear based on the mugshot of the late FatherGod that Royal was his son, but his bloodline didn't make me like the nigga in the slightest.

"Okay, and? Am I supposed to be impressed?" I asked, giving Carrie her phone back.

"Nah, nothing like that. I just wanted you to know who this dude was because it's obvious he's a part of Tesha's life. I'm assuming this was the guy who was coming from Africa to see her," she replied.

"If the nigga got the juice like that then he can help us get Ty back," Nyaisha said quickly.

"We don't need that bitch muthafucka's help," I growled, storming off in the direction of my bedroom.

It was beyond my comprehension why no one could see the danger in bringing in a new nigga to this situation, but it was obvious that all these bitches were too trusting. Tesha couldn't have known this nigga for more than five minutes, so to me, it was insane to trust him with sensitive information that could get us locked up or killed. If I was forced to drop a body in front of him then it was a safe bet that I'd drop his ass right beside it with no remorse. The only people that I trusted with my secrets at this point were myself and my wife. This nigga, Royal, wasn't on the guest list of known or trusted associates either, so I had no use for him personally. I could feel a tension headache coming on, and the jet lag definitely wasn't helping it, but I knew there was no time for a nap. I would have to settle for a shower instead, so I made sure that the water was hot enough to cook a jailhouse noodle. After stripping off my clothes, I mentally cleared my mind as I stepped under the blistering wave of water and let it beat my fatigue into submission. It didn't take long before I started to feel like myself a little bit, and that allowed me to work on a plan in my mind from several angles. By the time my shower was over, I had a to-do list taking shape with clear vision, and I headed back into my bedroom with more pep in my step. The sight of Carrie sitting on my bed made me pull up short though. Her attention had been on her phone's screen, but as soon as she heard me and looked up, my naked body had her undivided attention.

"What are you doing?" I asked.

"I, uh, came to let you know that Nyaisha went to, uh, the hospital. I let her drive my truck."

"Okay," I replied, waiting on her to get up and leave the room.

She didn't move though, and her eyes roamed my entire body with the same appreciation that someone would have for a beautiful sunrise. I was trying to behave, but she was making my dick hard, and I couldn't exactly hide it from her.

"Carrie?"

"Huh?"

"You're staring," I said, chuckling.

"Yeah, I guess I am. Wouldn't you though if the roles were reversed?"

My mind flashed back to the night she'd gotten me out of jail, which was the first time I'd seen her, and I had admired her beauty then myself. Right now though, her question was a loaded one if I'd ever heard one, but the sound of my phone ringing put a hold on any immediate answer I might've given. I moved to retrieve my pants that were on the floor by my bed, and I pulled my phone out of my pocket.

"Hey, Uncle, where are..."

My question was interrupted by the frantic sound of my uncle's voice giving me very simple instructions. Before I could get another word out, the line went dead in my ear, leaving me looking at the phone in confusion.

"What happened?" she asked, standing up.

"I don't know... but we've gotta go."

"Go? Go where?" she asked, confused.

I ignored her questions for the moment and went into my closet to put on some clothes. My mind was moving with the speed of a fighter jet engine even though I had no idea what was going on. Umar's words were still ringing in my ear, and he'd been clear about this location no longer being safe.

He'd instructed us to run, and that was what we would do. I came out of the closet to find Carrie in the same spot, and that pissed me off for some reason.

"Carrie, we gotta go so grab your shit and…"

My instructions were interrupted by the power suddenly going out around us, and I felt my stomach drop instantly. No power meant no security and no surveillance, which added up to one thing in my mind. The wolves were coming.

Chapter 4

(Royal)

"Dr. Westlake, how long will it be before I'm healed up?" Tesha asked.

"Well, that all depends on your body honestly. So far, you've shown that your body can withstand substantial trauma and remain almost completely intact. Most people that I've treated for gunshot wounds while being pregnant lose the baby immediately, but your little girl is a fighter, just like her mom. I expect you to make it to full term. You need plenty of rest and relaxation though, and most of all, no more bullets looking to call your body home. I've prescribed you pain medications that won't harm your baby and a fast-acting antibiotic to prevent any infection inside where the bullet hit your lung. Your immediate surgery when you first arrived here took care of any concerns that I might've had, so all in all, I'd say you're on a quick road to recovery."

Hearing the doctor say all of this was music to my ears because it allowed me to put my next moves into play sooner than later. I could tell that Tesha had been paying attention to what the doctor said, but the dazed look on her face right now signaled her mind being elsewhere.

"T, you good?" I asked, taking a step away from the wall and back over to her bedside.

"A g-girl? Did he say that I was having a little girl?" she asked, looking up at me with a panic-stricken expression.

"No, what he said is that WE'RE having a little girl," I replied, taking her hand in my own and giving it a comforting squeeze.

The smile that she gave me spoke gratitude and love combined with the beauty that always made my heart beat faster.

"Doctor, when can she leave the hospital?" Tonya asked from across the room.

"Well, that's hard to say. She's not in any life-threatening danger right now but monitoring her here for a few days is standard procedure. It's really up to the patient at this point, but as her doctor, I recommend another forty-eight hours here."

The doctor and Tonya were looking at Tesha, but Tesha was looking up at me to assist with the next decision.

"Doctor Westlake, we really appreciate your help, and we'd like time to discuss out options," I said politely.

The doctor took the hint and left without saying another word. No one spoke at first, and I got the feeling that Tesha and Tonya were waiting on me to speak first.

"You know that it's not gonna be long before Roland and his people know that you're not dead, right? Once that happens, you move higher up on the liability list, especially because you're one of the few people who knows that he ain't dead."

"But I didn't see him, so how would he know that I know anything?" Tesha asked logically.

"Because paranoia is a powerful thing, and it would be real easy for him to assume that if you ain't dead then you must've heard him speaking. The bottom line is that he can't afford to leave you alive, and I'd be surprised if whoever is in charge of Zoe Pound didn't order Roland to find you and kill you. Or be killed himself," I replied.

The fear in her eyes was instant, changing the emerald coloring into a jade green that was no less beautiful.

"The longer you stay here, Tesha, the easier it'll be to find you, so I think we should leave," Tonya said.

"And go where, Ma? It's obvious that we've underestimated these muthafuckas' reach, resources, and resolve to see our Black asses dead!"

"Easy, baby, just breathe," I said, sitting beside her on the bed and taking her other hand in mine.

I waited to speak again until she'd visibly calmed down, and the monitors that she was hooked up to showed that her heart rate was close to normal.

"Tesha, I know that you can feel how much I fuck with you, even if we ain't said all the cute words yet. I got you, bae, and that's on God. I promise that any nigga or bitch coming for you gotta go through me and mine, and I guarantee that we're hard to handle. I've already set some things in motion, so all you gotta do is trust me, and I'll have you somewhere safe within the hour," I vowed.

"Royal, you know that I trust you, and I'm just as fucked up about you as you are me, but what about everyone else? I can't just leave my family to the wolves while you whisk me away to whatever paradise you have waiting."

"I wouldn't suggest anything like that, and your family can come with us. Including David," I replied genuinely.

"He'd never agree to that, and besides, where we live is the safest place in the world right now," Tonya said.

"Until it's not," I countered, knowing how the opps could move to create vulnerability.

"My ma is right. David would never run while his wife is out there somewhere, but I do think it's time to admit that we're liabilities right now. How can I expect anyone to hunt Roland down if they're constantly worried about me? Ma, the same goes for your pregnant ass too."

"Wait, what about your baby's daddy? Will you be safe with him?" I asked, looking at Tonya.

"Tesha, don't," Tonya immediately said.

"It's okay, Ma. I trust Royal, and I know he ain't the judgmental type."

"Oh, I'm definitely not the nigga to judge because I've got a closet full of skeletons. It did surprise me that you, your mom, and your twin were all pregnant at the same time. I can't even lie. That's some shit for the *Maury* show," I said, chuckling.

"More like the *Jerry Springer* show," Tesha mumbled.

"What do you mean?" I asked curiously.

Tesha and her mom shared a strange look that didn't answer my question in the slightest, but I was prepared to move on in the conversation.

"David is my baby's father too," Tonya blurted out.

I could feel my jaw go slack, which indicated that my mouth was hanging open, but there was nothing I could do about it. I was literally mind blown.

"Stop playing," I finally said, looking back and forth between the women.

"She's not playing," Tesha said unflinchingly.

I understood with the quickness that there was nothing I could say about this nigga getting his wife, her sister, and her momma pregnant that wouldn't sound fucked up, so I kept it pushing.

"Well, with you being pregnant, I think it's a good idea for you to go with Tesha."

"And where exactly would we be going?" Tesha asked.

"I've got some good hiding spots. Don't worry," I replied, flashing her a smile of devilish intent.

"Lead the way and I'll follow," she promised with unmistakable hunger in her eyes.

"Little girl, you're healing from being shot, so I'mma need you to get the dick off your brain," Tonya said.

The flush of shame that instantly heated up Tesha's skin tone made me laugh, but I never let her hands go.

"Oh, my God, you're so embarrassing, Ma!"

"Thank you," Tonya said, laughing.

The lighthearted moment eased the awkward tension in the room, and I knew it was time to make shit happen.

"Tonya, I need you to tell the doctor to start the paperwork for Tesha's discharge while I arrange for our escort."

When she looked at Tesha to get her opinion, all she got was a smile, but that was all the answer she needed because she left the room quietly.

"Are you really not gonna tell me where we're going?" she asked.

"Absolutely not."

"Royal!" she whined, giving me a sexy pout that made me lightheaded.

I pulled my phone out and started shooting orders through text, just to avoid eye contact and break the spell that she had on me. The way my name escaped her lips was poetry to my ears, and it weakened my resolve.

"Royal?"

"Huh?"

"Baby, come here. I need to tell you something," she whispered softly.

When I looked up at her, I saw trouble spelled in all capital letters, but that didn't stop me from scooting closer to her. I leaned down until our faces were inches apart, which allowed her to cup my face and pull my lips to hers. The moment our mouths touched, it felt like I'd forgotten how to breathe, but within seconds, she was doing it for both of us. Her tongue greeted mine like old friends with boundary issues, and she tasted like warm caramel candy melting fast on my taste buds. The power that she wielded with her mouth forced me into unconscious surrender so suddenly that it took me a few moments to realize that my eyes were still closed after the kissing stopped. I was startled when I opened them, but she was looking at me with so much love that I couldn't be embarrassed.

"We're leaving the country, and that's all I'm telling you," I said, pulling back and returning to my phone.

Her laughter was sweet, even though it caused her to wince a little in pain. An incoming text diverted my attention, but it was good news that made me smile.

"So, the private security firm that I've used before will provide round the clock service for you, and they'll be here within the hour. Once they get here, we can..."

My thought was changed by a sound that was distant but completely unmistakable.

"Was that a gun going off?" she asked.

My response was to pull my own gun out and quickly cross the room to the door leading into the hallway. I took a fast peek around the corner, and I saw Tonya backing her way down the hall toward this room while shooting at someone I couldn't see. I made a move to step into the hallway and help, but two bullets lifted Tonya off of her feet and slid her into a nearby wall. I could see death on her face from where I stood, and fear gripped me because I never wanted to see Tesha like that.

"Royal!"

I moved back toward Tesha's bed to quiet her hysterics, passing her my pistol as I grabbed her bag and tossed it inside of mine that had been sitting in the corner of the room. All that she had in the world was in her bag, and I knew she'd need it later on. I hadn't known what to expect when I landed earlier, so I'd arranged to travel safely, and right now, I was glad for my paranoia.

"Listen to me, baby. I want you to shoot anyone who walks into this room. I'm going out here to buy us some time," I said, loading the hundred round drum on my fully automatic Glock .19.

"Wh-What's going on? Where's my mom?"

"No questions, Tesha. Just be ready to shoot if you have to and I'll be right back," I replied.

"Wait, no. Royal, you can't leave me!"

Her distress was obvious, and it pulled at my heart, but I pushed my emotions down because they were an indulgence that would get both of us killed.

"Tesha, I'll never leave you. I promise. I love you," I said sincerely.

I didn't wait for her to respond. I simply turned and headed back toward the door. When I peeked back down the hall, I saw four cops slowly advancing in my direction, and I almost felt relief. Then, one of them pumped two more bullets through Tonya's skull, and any notion I had of them being saviors went out the window with her brain matter. It was up to me, and that thought made me smile as I stepped around the corner with my gun up and ready. Killing was an old business for me, and business was always good.

Chapter 5

(Tynesha)

I could see the gun shaking in his hand, almost as if he was struggling to keep it pressed to my forehead because of its weight. The expression of shock and disbelief on his face was classically comical, but I didn't laugh because I knew instinctively that I had him where I wanted him.

"Y-You're pregnant, Ty? Like for real pregnant?"

"It's very real. I'm carrying your son but don't let that stop you from shooting me," I replied nonchalantly.

He waited a few more seconds, and then, he lowered the gun to his side. The fact that he didn't put it away and the suspicion that I could see taking shape in his eyes let me know that he wasn't completely sold yet. The hook was in his mouth though, which meant that I only had to pull in order to lock that bitch in his jaw.

"For someone so smart, Roland, I really don't understand how you didn't figure this part out sooner. You and I had been together for years, fighting and making up, and the last fight that we'd had that day that I left wasn't anything different than before. What made it different for me was the fact that I knew I was pregnant, and I refused to let you beat my baby out of me. I refused to let him grow up and be like you, which meant that I couldn't raise him with you the way that you were. I knew that you wouldn't change if I didn't make you change because we both know that I'd begged you to do it before. Leaving was my only option. I just so happened to run into David that day, and you decided to show your ass in public at the gas station. You made him my protector, but you also gave me a way out because I knew exactly what kind of nigga David was and ultimately what he would do. So, I confided in him about you and why I ran away, and as predicted, he stepped in on some Captain Save-a-Hoe type shit. Everything that happened after that was your doing. This whole time, you thought that I left you and fell in love with another nigga when I was really just trying to keep YOUR kid safe. It's fitting that him and I die by your hand though, so by all means, put the gun back to my head and pull the trigger. Pussy."

The last word from my mouth was spoken with disgust and a smile that I could tell was infuriating to him, but I knew that he wouldn't do anything now. I'd been watching him the whole time I was talking, and I knew the explanation I'd given made too much sense to him, especially given the fact that he was still upset with me. Those feelings were just one of the many things he couldn't hide with his new face because it was all in his eyeballs. I could see the wheels turning, and I could smell the wood burning, which meant that he was thinking hard as fuck right now. It was the perfect time to play on his emotional havoc.

"Why couldn't you just be a normal nigga? You could've been a great f-father if you just..."

I intentionally left the sentence hanging between us as I turned my back to him and took several breaths like I was fighting to maintain my composure.

"Ty, I didn't... I mean, if I had known then, I could've been different, and we could've worked together. You running didn't help though, and now... Shit. Now, I don't even know what to think."

"You don't believe me?!" I accused, spinning around to face him with fire in my eyes.

The surprise on his face told me that I'd hit the nail on the head, but this was something that I'd suspected, so I didn't feel any panic.

"Go get me a pregnancy test and I'll pee on the damn stick in front of your muthafuckin ass," I said with clear determination and annoyance.

The immediate smirk that appeared on his face told me that he liked the idea I'd thrown out there, but I'd known that he would.

"A pregnancy test, huh? Okay, but I'm not taking you with me so move that way," he demanded, pointing up the stairs with his pistol.

The hesitation in my steps was real because I had no idea want awaited up those stairs, but I moved up them anyway. When I got to the top of the stairs, there was a short hallway that led to the one door on this floor.

"Keep going," he demanded, giving me a gentle push with his hand.

My feet moved slow, but my mind was running like an Indy car chasing the checkered flag. I analyzed every word I'd just spoken to him downstairs, looking for any holes or cracks in my story, but I found none. Either way, there was no going back, so I mentally settled into the role I was about to play. I opened the door and stepped into a dimly lit room that smelled faintly musty with a hint of new paint. The only furniture was a queen-sized bed attached to a black, metal, canopy style frame with a matching headboard.

"Lay on the bed."

"What?!" I asked, whirling around and looking at the nigga like he'd lost his damn mind.

"Forcing sex on you ain't never been my thing so stop looking at me like that and lay your simple ass down," he said, raising his gun in a threatening way.

It was hard to resist the urge to press my luck, but I did resist just that, and I laid down on top of the all-white comforter.

"Now put your hands over your head," he instructed, tucking his gun and pulling more zip ties from his pocket.

Again, I complied, and within moments, he had my hands and wrists secured firmly to the headboard.

"Comfy?" he asked, stepping back and admiring his handiwork.

"Oh, yeah, this is great."

My sarcasm made him chuckle, but I could tell that he was secretly proud of himself.

"I'm gonna go pick up a pregnancy test, and then, we'll see what the truth is for real. Do you need me to get you anything else while I'm out?"

This question would seem normal, considerate even, if it weren't for the fact that I was strapped to a fucking bed by a nigga with bad intentions.

"I need you to text my mom and tell her to get the fuck out of that building. She's pregnant too, and you already killed Tesha and her baby so..."

"I killed your sister. I didn't kill any fucking kid!" he stated heatedly.

I didn't say anything, but my eyes stayed locked in on his face as I waited patiently. After about half a minute, the lights behind his eyes burned brighter due to the winds of common sense blowing through his brain.

"Tesha was… She was pregnant?" he asked in a voice that was hollowed out by horror.

"Yeah, my twin was pregnant and excited about having her first child, but you took that from her when you shot her for no damn reason. I'm asking you not to let my mother suffer the same fate because if you do, I swear on the soul of my child that I'll never forgive you."

I could tell by the look of uncertainty in his eyes that he knew my statement was as true as the gospel, but I didn't know if that was enough to make him do the right thing.

"We can talk about this after you take the pregnancy test," he said, turning and heading for the door.

"It could be too late, Roland! You were the one who spoke like whatever was gonna happen was imminent so don't bullshit like there's all the time in the world now! Please, Roland."

I hated to beg this nigga for anything other than for him to die a painful and brutal death, but pride wasn't a luxury that I could afford right now. All I cared about was saving the rest of my family.

"Look, Tynesha, I..."

The sound of Rick Ross rapping froze his sentence and had him digging his phone out of his pocket. He answered the call, but he never spoke a word. He simply listened with a blank expression on his face. After a few moments, he disconnected the call and stood there in the middle of the floor, staring at me. The uneasiness I was feeling traveled from my brain down to the pit of my stomach faster than thunder could follow lightening.

"What is it? Why are you looking at me like that?" I asked, tasting fear fill my mouth with every drop of saliva that circulated.

"T-Tesha is still alive. She survived my shots, and she's in the hospital."

It was impossible to describe the immense relief that washed over me like summer rain, but a nagging worry remained because of the look on his face.

"What else? What aren't you telling me, Roland?" I asked while mentally bracing for impact.

It seemed like he was staring through me until his eyes warmed back up a few degrees and locked in on my face.

"Y-You were right, Ty. You were right when you said that Zoe Pound would be the only winners in the end, but I didn't know that until now. I didn't know until they cut me off and basically told me that I was a dead man just as soon as they could arrange it."

His revelation didn't create any joy in my heart, and maybe it was just because of how lost he looked in that moment. Even though he technically wasn't a member, Zoe Pound was all that Roland had known since he was a kid. Those doors were now closed to him, and that meant that part of his identity had effectively been stripped from him. One thing that I knew for sure was that this turn of events made him more dangerous than he'd been a moment ago.

There was little doubt in my mind that, right now, he was feeling like he had nothing and no one to live for. That meant that he didn't have shit to lose, and I needed to change that perspective before it grew roots in his mind.

"I know that it don't seem like it right now, but they just did you a favor. There would be no way for us to raise a baby around Zoe Pound and their bullshit. Would you really want your daughter to go through something like this?" I asked, jerking with my bound hands to demonstrate what I meant.

At first, he didn't respond, but then, he got an odd look in his eyes that I didn't understand or like.

"Daughter? I thought you said you were carrying my son," he said, pulling his pistol out and aiming it at my stomach.

"I-I did say that, and I am carrying your son, but we'd always talked about having more kids than one, right?"

"So what you saying? Am I supposed to believe that you suddenly wanna raise a family with me?" he asked skeptically.

"If you've changed then that's exactly what I'm saying, but if not then you can just shoot us now."

He didn't lower his gun, but his eyes did move downward to my stomach, and he seemed to be studying my body. Thank God for the fact that I was showing already because, right now, there was nothing else to combat this nigga's doubt. I made sure to add emphasis to my baby bump by pushing my stomach out as much as I could while maintaining the appearance of normal breathing.

"Life on the run is no type of life for a baby, and you know that. Kids need stability, and we can't guarantee that," he said somberly.

"There are few guarantees in life, Roland, and nobody's parents are perfect. We'll be fine though. Just untie me and let's get the fuck out of here before some of them Zoe Pound niggas show up."

"You make it sound so easy, Ty, but it's not. It's just not," he said, moving the gun away from my stomach up toward my head.

I opened my mouth to speak, but he fired two quick shots that silenced me.

Chapter 6

(David)

"David?" Carrie whispered.

"Shhh, just stay where you are," I replied, backing into my closet and going to the safe.

Thankfully, it was connected to its own power source, and the keypad was now lit neon green to guide me to it like a beacon. I quickly opened it while grabbing a laundry bag off the floor next to it, and then, I emptied the contents inside. My matching pearl handled Smith & Wesson .45s with their thirty-three round clips were kept out as I pulled the drawstring on the bag and reached for the gun that I kept on top of the safe.

"David?" Carrie whispered again.

When I looked over to where the sound of her voice was, I saw her standing at the closet door, holding her phone close to her face and using the light on it to see.

"Take this," I said, holding out one of the pistols and the laundry bag.

She moved without hesitation and quickly slipped the bag around her back before taking the pistol.

"Do you know how to shoot?" I asked.

Her response was to check the chamber to make sure there was a bullet on the VIP list, and then, she nodded with a smile. I threw the strap of the all-black Uzi over my arm and around my neck, adjusting it so that the gun aligned with my spine.

"Where are we going, David?"

If this was what I thought it was, then trying to make it downstairs to my car was sure to be a suicide mission. Undoubtedly, that was probably what the opps were expecting, and that was exactly why I would do the opposite. "We're going up," I replied, grabbing the extra Uzi clip, putting it into my pocket, and leading the way out of the closet.

The .45 in my grip gave me comfort, but my nerves were still bad because I knew that a dog fight was coming. Night was just taking a firm hold outside of my bedroom, but the stars allowed enough light to shine through to make seeing our path possible. I knew once we were in the hallway and stairway, we'd face pitch blackness, and that was an unequal playing field. For that reason, I stopped in the kitchen and grabbed a flashlight from the drawer, and then, we prepared to venture out into the unknown. My movements of opening the door and peering out into the hallway were done slowly and with extreme caution. I barely got a look around the corner of the door jam before the heat of flying bullets forced me back.

"Shit!" Carrie exclaimed.

"Turn around," I demanded while passing her my pistol.

I immediately loosened the drawstring on the bag and dug inside it until I felt what I was searching for and pulled them out. After pulling the string back tight, I turned her around.

"Get ready to run and shoot," I said, pulling both pins on the grenades clutched in my grip.

It took a few seconds before there was a lull in the shooting, but I wasted no time taking advantage of it by slinging the grenades down the hall. I quickly backed into the apartment, and a few seconds later, I felt the thunderous explosion rock the walls and shake the floor. Based on the short-lived screams, I knew the shooters who'd been trying to put my head on somebody's mantle over the fireplace were dead. I had no doubts that there were more on the premises though, and that was why not a second could be wasted in our escape.

"Come on," I said, reclaiming my gun and leading the way out into the hall.

I made a beeline for the stairway while firing blindly in the direction the shooters had occupied. Once we were secured inside the stairway, I was taking the steps two at a time, running, heading for higher ground. We ran the six flights, making it to the roof fast enough to make the U.S. Olympic track team envious. As I'd expected, there were no shooters up here, only the helicopter that belonged to one of the building's tenants. Whoever that tenant was, they were about to be pissed.

"Do you know how to fly?" Carrie asked fearfully.

"Sure, we had choppers in the hood all my life. How hard could it really be?"

"You'd be surprised, but luckily for you, I used to fuck a pilot once upon a time. I'll fly; you shoot," she said, handing me the gun she'd been clutching.

She swiftly climbed up into the helicopter while I positioned myself against the wall next to the door leading to the roof. I didn't know how long it would take her to be ready to take off, but I knew the odds were good that the remaining building security operatives had already figured out where we were. Having to shut down the power in the building was a gift and a curse for whoever had done it, and they probably knew that now. They thought that they could catch me sleeping, and now, the tables had turned hella fast because they couldn't see me lurking. I thought that I could hear the faint sounds of boots on the steps, but the sudden whine of the chopper's blades spinning drowned out everything.

I could see Carrie signaling me to get in, but I was focused on the door to my left and regulating my breathing. The whine of the blades grew louder as they spun faster, making it impossible to hear anything over them. I was almost convinced that my mind and my ears had been playing tricks on me from the beginning, and then, the door finally burst open beside me. Two men came barreling out, catching two head shots apiece from the guns in my grip and falling one on top of the other. I smoothly stepped over them and let more bullets fly into the darkness of the stairway before turning and sprinting for the helicopter. I hopped in and had just barely got the door pulled shut before she had us in the air, teetering like a clumsy baby. It seemed like we were only hovering in the air for a few seconds before we came to the edge of the building, and then, we fell in a straight nosedive.

"D-Do you know how to fly?" I yelled, dropping the guns in my lap so that I could put my seatbelt on.

"I'm trying to concentrate, David, so please keep the high pitches out of your voice."

The smile on her face made me want to push her ass out of the helicopter but watching her work the stick between her legs told me how easy this was not. It seemed like we fell for an eternity before we finally levelled off and shot forward into the night sky. Something in me compelled my eyes to look backwards, and the massive silhouette of the blacked-out building had never looked more threatening. This was the second time that I'd had to abandon a place I considered home, and that shit was unacceptable. I needed to plan and strategize better, but first, I had to figure out who and what I was planning for. That search started with my uncle because it was obvious that he knew enough to give us that heads up before death showed her beautiful smile. I tapped Carrie on the shoulder to get her attention.

"We need to get to the hospital," I said loudly.

"Already ahead of you."

I followed the finger that she was pointing with, and I saw the hospital's helipad outside of my window in the distance. Since Nyaisha was already there with Tonya and Tesha, we would all hop in Carrie's SUV and become invisible. Within a few minutes, we were close enough to the hospital for me to see people in the windows, but my eyes were on the ground outside. There were red and blue lights flashing, which meant police, not ambulances. My heartbeat increased because, in my soul, I knew that something had happened here tonight as well. Something that couldn't be undone. The only thing that I could think was that Royal better not have let Tesha get killed, or his ass was mine.

"What do you wanna do?" she asked, clearly seeing the same things out her window as I was.

"Land us."

"David, you know that if the cops recognize you then the only way you walk out of there is in handcuffs, right?"

"Yeah, I know, but I don't have a choice. Land us," I instructed again.

She nodded, and within a few minutes, we were parked beside the hospital's chopper. Once the blades had stopped spinning, I reclaimed my backpack from her and put all of my guns inside.

"Act natural and follow me," I said, pushing the door open and hopping out.

We made our way to the stairway door and walked down one flight before coming into the hospital as casually as we could. I took her hand in mine and headed for the nearest nurse's station to find the answers we would need.

"Excuse me, nurse? I'm trying to visit a friend that is on the third floor, and…"

"Oh, I'm sorry, sir, but no one is allowed on that floor right now because the cops have it locked down. If you will please be patient then I'm sure you will be able to see your friend soon," the nurse politely explained.

Carrie and I exchanged a quick look that revealed our similar thought pattern.

"Thank you so much," I said, turning and walking away.

I led Carrie down the corridor until I found an empty room to pull her into so that we could gather our thoughts.

"This ain't no coincidence, David."

"I'm already knowing. What I'm not understanding is how the fuck the opps got the upper hand so fast."

"I don't know either. What did your uncle say back at the apartment?" she asked, pulling her phone out.

"Not much. He just said that the building wasn't safe for us anymore and that we needed to get out immediately."

"How is that even possible though? From what I understand, that building and the people who live in it are like citizens of a foreign country who protect each other. In order for them to turn on you like that means somebody powerful is working behind the scenes," she concluded.

"You're right, and we need to know who that is, but right now, we need to find a way to check on Tesha."

"I'm calling Nyaisha now," she replied, swiftly dialing a number and waiting on an answer.

When she put it on speaker, I heard it ring half a dozen times before her voice finally came on the line.

"Yo?"

"Aye, Nyaisha, where you at?" I asked.

"At the fucking hospital, bro, but them faggot ass cops won't let me in because they say some shit went down. Like an active shooter type situation."

"They not saying who was shot?" I asked, holding my breath.

"Nah, they ain't saying shit, but I put the pretty brown eyes on this husky nigga working security, and he spilled the tea that he had. Some shit popped off on Tesha's floor, but they not saying no names about who got hit. All I know is that it was multiple people shot, and Tesha not in her hospital room."

"Where the fuck is she?" Carrie asked before I could.

"I don't know, but my money is on the nigga, Royal, that you told me about because from what I heard, that nigga ain't here neither."

The relief I felt was quickly overshadowed by the irritation to my soul over that nigga being involved in any way, but I kept my comments to myself. As long as Tesha and the baby were safe, that was all that mattered. At least that was what I thought until I remembered who else had been in Tesha's room when I left.

"Nyaisha, what about Tonya?" I asked.

"I don't know, but my best guess is that she's with Tesha and Royal. I'm about to leave and come back to your apartment so that we..."

"Nah, the apartment ain't safe no more. We're in the hospital on the fifth floor right now, but we'll meet you in the ER lobby in a few minutes," I said, hanging up before she could speak again.

"What do you think, David?"

"Honestly, I don't know what to think. I just know that we need to regroup because we can't fight without balance. They caught us by surprise, but that shit won't happen again."

"Okay, well, I'm with you," she replied.

"Listen, Carrie, you don't gotta take this trip with us because there's no telling how many more people might die before it's all said and done."

"I'm with you," she said again, squeezing my hand in hers.

Arguing with her seemed like a waste of valuable time, so I chose to accept her help graciously and move on.

"Let's go," I said, leading the way out of the room and back to the stairway.

It took us almost ten minutes to make it downstairs and to the ER on the other side of the hospital, but Nyaisha was right there waiting on us.

"Where did you park?" Carrie asked.

"In the lot on the side of the building but we've got a problem."

"What's that?" I asked, already bracing for emotional impact.

"It's T-Tonya. She's dead."

Chapter 7

(Royal)

Innocent bystanders could be heard screaming as bullets flew up and down the hallway, but I was numb to whatever they were feeling. My sole focus was my finger on the trigger while the hundred round drum on my Glock moved with the sex appeal of a bitch shaking her muthafuckin ass. The first four cops went down in a hurry, bringing more honor to the badge on their chest now that they were dead than when they were living. Two more cops tried to get off a clean shot from around a corner, forcing me to alter my shots and knock holes in the wall's plaster in order to drop them. I stopped firing long enough to listen, but my feet kept moving forward, staying in sync with my eye's left to right sweeping motion. I grabbed the walkie talkie off of the first dead cop that I came to, and I tucked it in my back pocket. I wanted to do the decent thing by taking Tonya with us, but I settled for dragging her body out of the hallway and into a hospital room so that Tesha wouldn't see her like this. The seconds that were passing grew louder in my mind, forcing me to move faster. I was vigilant for anymore shooters or potential threats as I made my way back to Tesha's room. I could taste the thick gun smoke wafting on the air in the hallway, but it still wasn't enough to cover the smell of blood and death that these corridors would forever be known for. My body had a familiar tingle to it, and I suddenly realized that I'd been missing this kind of action in the quiet last few years. I consciously made sure that this joy of feeling alive wasn't visible on my face though as I went to Tesha's room.

"T, it's me coming in," I announced to avoid getting shot.

I moved slow until I saw the terror on her face, and then, I was damn near running to her bedside.

"Wh-What the hell happened? Where's my mom?"

I couldn't bring myself to answer that question around the lump that the truth had put in my throat. I knew the pain that she was getting ready to feel, and I wouldn't wish that on anyone except for my enemies.

"Royal... tell me," she insisted, already fighting against the cracking in her voice.

All I could manage to do was look her in the eyes, but that was enough. Her tears fell from what seemed like an endless height, and it was like watching a sad silent film that made my heart ache to give her comfort. There would be time for that part though once we were safe. I spotted a wheelchair in the room across the hall, and I quickly went to get it before returning to her bedside.

"Come on, baby. We gotta go," I said gently while my fingers moved swiftly to unhook her from the hospital's machines.

When that was done, she took my gun so that I could lift her from the bed and place her in the wheelchair. After she was seated, I grabbed my bag and passed it to her before pushing her toward the door. Once I made sure the coast was clear, I wheeled her out into the hallway nice and calmly, heading in the opposite direction of the murder and mayhem.

"Were those c-cops?" she asked.

"Yeah, but they were dirty and obviously sent here as a cleanup crew."

She didn't say anything more about that, and I kept us moving toward the bank of elevators at the end of the hall. We got on board, and I hit the button that would take us to the parking structure that was attached to the hospital. We made it to the dark blue Maserati that I'd rented when I'd known that I was going to have to put boots on the ground without having to shoot anyone else. The police radio in my back pocket was still silent too, which told me that for the moment, there weren't more assassins in blue uniforms roaming the building. I got Tesha loaded up into the car before running around to the driver side and getting behind the wheel. Within a few minutes, we were exiting the parking structure, and I could hear the sounds of sirens rolling in waves through the fast-approaching nightfall. Naturally, I headed in the opposite direction of their approach, although I had no actual destination in mind. When I looked over at Tesha with the intentions of asking where we should go, I found her with her head back against the headrest and waterfalls leaking from beneath her closed eyelids. That prevented me from speaking, and it also left the ball in my court about which way to go. Her mom was dead, and her twin had been abducted, so there was no doubt that she felt more alone than she ever had before. I knew that feeling and the utter despair that accompanied it intimately, and I would've given anything to take her pain as my own.

"People tell you all the time that they know how you feel when it comes to heartache or loss, and most of the time, they know that their words are meaningless. A hollow platitude that someone found in a fortune cookie and then passed it along like it was the gospel. From the beginning, I promised you that we wouldn't bullshit each other, so I won't start now by telling you that I know exactly what you're feeling in this moment. I have an idea though. My mom was murdered seven years ago... by my big sisters."

My revelation made her open her eyes and look at me, but I kept my eyes on the road because it was still painful to speak on this subject.

"The story is long and colorful about how shit got to that point, but the big picture is that I lost my mother at the hands of three women that I've come to love very much. I didn't meet my sisters until I was eleven years old, so I didn't understand their relationship or the horrifying history that they shared with our mother. In my eyes, my mother had no demons, and if she did, I still wouldn't have gave a fuck because she was all I had in this world. In an instant, I lost her and gained the most dysfunctional family on planet earth. We all came to grow to love and respect each other, but there's not a single day that passes when I don't miss my mother," I confessed.

She continued to stare at me, but she didn't say anything at first. A sign for a Marriott hotel caught my eye, and I quickly pulled into the parking lot so that we could plan our next move.

"How did you forgive your sisters? I know that you're close to them now, but still... how?"

"I had to learn the hard way that sometimes we do shit that makes things unavoidable. Our mother put herself in a few of those fucked up situations where shit happens, and it became impossible for her not to meet karma. I didn't understand that until my own decisions caused me to get my little brother's mom killed. She died because of me, and one day, I'll have to expose that ugly truth to him, and in that moment, I'll only want one thing. Forgiveness," I replied honestly.

When she reached over and took my hand in hers, I finally looked at her, and the understanding that I saw allowed a single tear to slide down my face.

"I love you, Royal, and I truly appreciate the man that you've become."

I pulled her hand to my lips and kissed the back of it before looking back through the windshield. We sat there, holding hands in silence, letting our emotions feed off of each other in a way that allowed pain to comfort pain without demanding answers that didn't exist. I'd told her a lot about myself in the time we'd spent getting to know one another, but I'd kept the truth about my mother a secret for several reasons. The main one being how emotionally vulnerable it left me feeling. Now that it was out in the open, I felt like I'd finally found the person that I could bare my soul to, and that brought me peace.

"There's more ugliness in my past, but I promise to do everything in my power not to let these demons hurt you or our beautiful baby girl."

"I know you will, but even if that does happen, because life is funny sometimes, I'm still here for all of it. We'll figure out life together. Does that sound okay to you?"

"Sounds like the best thing I've ever heard," I replied, pulling her toward me so that I could kiss her tears away.

She folded into my arms as comfortably as if she'd been there her whole life, and in my heart, I knew that this was the perfect place for her to be. After a while, she pulled back a little and looked up at me, still beautiful as her tears continued to fall.

"What do we do now?" she asked.

"We regroup and fight back. The trick to succeeding with that tactic is to fight back on our terms when we're completely ready, and the opps can't counter our moves in time to survive. I won't lie to you though, bae. The pain that you're feeling now will get worse at times, and it'll make you say fuck having patience. To be patient is the only way to play this game at the same level as the masters, so we must suffer in silence for now."

"I understand what you're saying, but you're gonna have to help me," she said.

"Of course I will, without hesitation."

"Thank you, bae. So, what's our next move right now?" she asked, visibly gathering her composure.

"We need to link up with David and the rest of your people, and I need a place to work."

"Work? What do you mean?" she asked, confused.

"I may have forgot to mention that I've been computer hacking since I was a kid. I was taught by one of the best hackers in the world, and she gave me an education worth more than any ivy league institution of learning."

"Ah, so that's what you were talking about earlier when you and David got into it, and that's how you had the police find me," she said, nodding in clear understanding.

"Yeah, that's it. And that's how I'm gonna shift the advantage so that we can play more offense than defense. We need a safe place to lay low though, and I'm hoping that David will know of one since we're in his city."

"After what just happened, and the fact that it was the cops who did it protecting one of their own, I don't think there's anywhere safe in the entire state of Florida right now. We need to link up with David, Carrie, and Nyaisha and then follow the plan you were hinting at in the hospital," she stated.

"I hear you, but what if David won't come with us?"

"Then that's his choice, and he's a grown ass man," she replied seriously.

I knew that I couldn't begin to understand the complexities of their relationship, but it was good to know that she had her priorities straight when it came to him. I pulled my phone out of my pocket and passed it to her so that she could make the call.

"I'm surprised that you don't have this muthafucka encrypted, Mr. Hacker."

"Who said it wasn't?" I asked, chuckling.

The small smile that she gave me was a much-needed improvement from the pain that had been displayed across her beauty. I continued to study her facial features as she talked to David, and it was easy to tell early on that the nigga was still being difficult. I wanted so bad to grab the phone and tell the nigga to stop being a bitch, but I knew that would only make him more hostile and cause him to say some shit that he would have to answer for. It was more productive to let her handle it, but the expression on her face told me that her patience with him had run its course. When she hung up the phone without a word, she let out a long, frustrated sigh before laying her head against my chest.

"Talk to me, T."

"That nigga won't get out of the way of his pride and make the smart decision, and I've never seen him move like this. Losing Ty and now my mom has him all fucked up."

I didn't mention the fact of losing her too, at least from an emotional standpoint, but I knew that was a big issue for him right now with me in the equation.

"What did he say?" I asked.

"That he's taking Nyaisha back to New York and then going underground. He plans to handle shit his way as soon as he gets in touch with his uncle."

"Okay, so while he does that, we'll work on shit from our end, and when the time comes, we'll meet in the middle. We all have the same goals, but David is just too emotional to see that," I said.

"Yeah, I guess you're right. As long as me, you, and the baby are safe, I'll be okay. Where do you wanna go?"

With David's lack of cooperation and my actions at the hospital, it was clear that Florida could now be considered one hundred percent enemy territory for us, so leaving was our only option. I wasn't trying to go far though, just far enough to be out of sight. I knew the perfect place to make that happen.

Chapter 8

(Tynesha)
(Two Weeks Later)
"Roland!" I yelled for the fifth time.

I knew that this nigga had to have heard me by now, even if he was downstairs and outside running the fucking chainsaw. Him not coming to see what I wanted was just his way of being funny with his petty ass. I started to say fuck it and simply piss on myself, which would force him to change the sheets and comforter on the bed, but I heard him finally coming. A few moments later, his heavy footsteps walked into the room, bringing his look of frustration into my field of vision.

"Ty, what the fuck do you want?"

"I gotta pee, nigga, because your son is dancing on my muthafuckin bladder!"

"You just peed like not even an hour ago, and you ain't drank a damn thing," he mumbled with irritation as he crossed the room to unlock the handcuffs holding me to the headboard.

It was on the tip of my tongue to remind this bitch ass nigga that we wouldn't be going through this if he would stop chaining me up like a damn dog. I bit back those words though and ran for the bathroom just as soon as my wrists were free. I barely got to plant my ass cheeks on the toilet seat before I felt my bladder explode like a burst pipe, but the satisfaction that I felt made it all worth it. When I was done, I made sure not to flush, just because I knew that it got on his nerves, and then, I washed my hands before going back into the bedroom. He was still standing by the bed with the handcuffs waiting, and for some reason, that made my blood hot enough for a good fight.

"Why the fuck are you keeping me handcuffed to the bed? I mean, you do realize that this stresses me out, which adds to the baby's stress level?"

"The baby will be fine. Now bring your ass over here," he demanded.

His words only succeeded in literally making me dig my heels in because this nigga must've forgotten that I'd take off on his ass.

"Roland, stop playing with me and talking to me like you go so hard because you don't. I saw the tears in your eyes when you read the results of the pregnancy test for yourself, and I know that you care about this baby. What we not bout to do is play with my intelligence just because you've got your panties in a bunch over the Zoe Pound situation."

The way that his expression changed told me that I'd hit the nail on the head when it came to identifying what had him emotionally unstable and not thinking straight. Ever since he'd gotten that call, he'd been erratic, to say the least. The fact that we were in the same house that he'd brought me to originally spoke to his suicidal tendencies. He insisted that Zoe Pound didn't know about this place, but I'd slept with one eye open knowing the reach and determination of them. Roland wasn't analyzing the situation like a nigga would who'd dealt with these people his whole life. I could smell his desperation, and it made me crave my husband even more.

"Tynesha, I've been real patient with you, but you're bout to piss me the fuck off with the dumb shit. There are several different ways this can go that result in the same outcome for me, but you will know pain and discomfort, or you can get your ass over here," he said with mounting frustration.

My feet moved of their own accord, carrying me in his direction, and right before we were standing toe to toe, I launched myself at his midsection. The sound of the air leaving his body in a rush gave me an exhilarating feeling of satisfaction, but I didn't waste time basking in it. Instead, I took a quick step back and fired a left right combination at his fat ass nose, landing both punches squarely. Instantly, his eyes began to water, reminding me of how he almost ugly cried during a drunken brawl we'd had one night, and that memory fed my anger more. The fact that I was back in this place of dysfunction with the same nothing ass nigga put the bitter taste of hatred in my mouth. The more I tried to swallow it, the more infected I became by it, and that translated into my hands moving faster. I managed to duck the lazy punch that he countered with, popping up on his left shoulder and firing an overhand right that knocked him into the bed. For a split second, I had the advantage, despite the size disadvantage, but that shifted before I could blink because I got tangled up in his legs when he fell on the bed. The result was him taking me to the mattress with him, and I immediately felt his forearm smash into the side of my head. My vision swam, but the fear that took ahold of me told me to stay away from those waves, forcing my knee to come up fast to try and move his nuts to his throat. I heard him yelp slightly from the blow that I landed, but I could tell that I hadn't hit him like I needed to because he still had the presence of mind to wrap his hands around my throat. My air supply was gone in a terrifying instant, and I'd been here before, so I knew that fighting back was useless, but that didn't stop me. I clawed at his hands until I felt his skin and blood under my fingernails, but his grip only became more punishing with its tightness.

"Baby," I croaked, trying to remind him that I was pregnant.

"You should've thought about that sooner," he whispered in my ear.

My vision was closing in on itself, and that was my last coherent thought before the darkness of being unconscious became my only friend. There was no dream like state for me to fall into. There was just nothing. The next thing that I knew, I was fighting for more breath as cold water returned me to the land of the living. Coughing and spitting the water out wasn't helping, and as soon as I opened my eyes, I realized that was because I was directly under the shower's spray. I quickly discovered that I could only move my head out of the way a little because the water was purposefully aimed at me, and I was handcuffed to the shower rod. It was hard work fighting against the instant panic within me, but I was finally able to do it and take stock of my situation. I was completely naked and vulnerable, and the expression on Roland's face told me just how much he was enjoying the view from his vantage point of leaning against the bathroom sink.

"G-Get m-me the f-f-fuck down," I demanded, beginning to shiver uncontrollably.

"Talk to me nicely, sweetheart. You know that I don't respond very well to you when your tone is disrespectful."

"F-Fuck you, pussy!" I replied, wishing that I could spit in his face.

"Is that an offer? Because if I remember correctly, the make-up sex after a fight like that would've left both of us delirious with satisfaction."

Everything in me wanted to tell him how many times I'd faked orgasms simply to get him and his little dick out of me, but I kept my mouth shut. Now wasn't the time to be a smartass. It was time to play nice before I caught pneumonia.

"R-R-Roland, g-get me d-d-down," I repeated, adjusting my tone to conceal as much of the hate that I felt as I could.

"Hold that thought," he replied, pulling his phone from his pocket.

I thought that he was either answering or making a phone call, but instead, the muthafucka started taking pictures of me. I wanted to scream every foul thing I'd ever thought or heard at this nigga, but my teeth were chattering too hard for those words to form. The only thing that I could do was brand this moment in time on my memory because if I ever got the opportunity to even the score, I was going to make sure to go up one. When he was finished humiliating me, he started texting someone, and my money was on it being David because I knew how petty Roland was. Not to mention the fact that the trap they'd laid for David and our family had been a complete shit show, catching no one in its clutches. When Roland had let that little piece of information out, I'd smiled inside, knowing that these muthafuckas had no idea what they'd just done. On a good day, David was the type of nigga that you had to kill because reasoning with him wasn't optional, but on a bad day... shit, that husband of mine was the gatekeeper to hell. I had no doubt that Zoe Pound and everyone connected to this situation was learning how formidable David was, but what they didn't realize yet was that he would not stop. Not ever. All I had to do was stay alive so that we could fight side by side again.

"R-Roland, please," I said, forcing my anger to remain calm.

His phone chimed, causing him to hold up a finger in my direction to put me on hold while he checked his texts. Even through the fog of borderline hypothermia, I could see the sickening, sinister smile spread widely across his face, and it reignited the fear in me. He stepped over to the shower and turned the water from cold to hot for a few minutes, and then, he turned it off. I was definitely still cold, but the brief hot shower stopped the shaking at least.

"I wanted you to know what I meant when I said that I saved your life," he said, sticking his phone in my face so that I could read his text messages. I immediately saw the pictures he'd taken of me and the message he attached to it that he'd give me to Zoe Pound as leverage over David. All he asked in return was to be allowed to keep breathing.

Before I even read the response, I knew what would be said, but actually seeing the words made my heart beat just a little harder.

"Y-You know they'll kill our baby if you do this, right? Is that what you want, Roland? If you want me and your baby dead, then why don't you do it yourself?"

"You know, Ty, you were right when you said that I care about that baby growing inside you, but these last two weeks, I keep coming back to the same question. Whose baby is it? You didn't lie about being pregnant, I'll give you that, but that still don't mean that your baby is biologically mine. You only look three to four months pregnant, and I would need you to be five to six months for me to believe that the kid is actually mine. Maybe not even then because you and David were fucking from day one like lifelong lovers so only a DNA test could convince me. Sadly, we don't have time for that because Zoe Pound is leaving no stone unturned looking for me, as well as your precious David. To my way of thinking, that leaves one of two options - save you and your baby or save me. Do you wanna guess what I'mma do, you ungrateful, spiteful bitch?"

For a full five seconds, my mind completely froze up because the panic and fear of what he was suggesting was just that overwhelming. Thankfully, my survival instincts kicked in, and I was allowed to breathe again while my mind adjusted at light speed.

"Honestly, Roland, I have no idea what you plan to do because I learned long ago that I never really knew you. I only knew what you projected. I THOUGHT that you'd never hurt a kid, any kid, but I guess I was wrong about that too. You don't have to claim your son or give him the love that so many little Black boys never know from their fathers. It's better that he's dead then because that neglect would only succeed in killing him slowly every day of his confused life. Give us to whoever and let them do what they're gonna do."

I could see the surprise that my words caused within him, but I was just praying that he couldn't hear my heart knocking against my rib cage. I had no idea what he would say, but before a word could leave his mouth, a foreign sound reached both of our ears, causing us to look in its direction. A vehicle had just pulled up.

Chapter 9

(David)
(Georgia)

"I got you something to eat," Carrie said, coming through the apartment door.

I didn't budge from my spot on the couch nor did I look away from the game of Call of Duty that I was playing.

"Did you hear me, David?"

"I heard you, and I'mma tell you like I told you earlier. I ain't hungry," I replied, dismissing her kind gesture with a wave of my hand.

This had more or less been our routine for the last couple weeks that we'd been holed up in Carrie's secret apartment. I was grateful for the place to hide, but sometimes, her desire to take care of me got on my nerves. In a short period of time, I'd learned that Carrie had incredible maternal instincts, and then, she'd told me the reason for that was because she had kids. It had surprised me because her 5'9", one hundred sixty pounds body looked flawless, so I had no idea how she'd had multiple kids. That surprise didn't last long though because her revelation about also being married was the shocker that had me looking at her sideways. Me and mine were out here in these streets on some do or die shit because those were the cards that were dealt to us, but Carrie was making a choice to fight this fight with us. That showed me how crazy loyal she was, and I could relate to her on that level.

"So, is your plan to just smoke, drink, and play video games until Tynesha miraculously pops up dead?" she asked.

"What the fuck you mean?"

"What I mean is that's all you've done since we got here. You're avoiding Dayjah and Shaomi. You've disobeyed your uncle, who told you to come back to Africa so that you could regroup. You're not eating, and you're barely sleeping. I'm just trying to understand what the fuck you've got going on because from where I'm standing, it ain't much," she replied seriously.

"I've got a plan, and I know what I'm doing. Leave me alone."

I felt like that was enough of an explanation to render our conversation over, but she obviously didn't believe that because she stepped right in front of the TV, blocking my view.

"A plan? Really? Break it down for a bitch real quick because, in case you forgot, I'm in this shit with your stubborn ass," she said with growing irritation.

"I'm making myself invisible and increasing the paranoia of the opps because they don't know where I am or when I'm coming. Eventually, this will cause them to either overcompensate or make a mistake, and when either of those things happens, death will be waiting. And it will be a savage ending fitting of all that I've lost."

Some time when I'd been speaking, the expression on her face had changed, softened a little, and then changed again to the concerned look she was wearing now. When she moved from in front of the TV, she came and sat next to me on the couch, setting the food on the coffee table in front of us.

"David, I feel like there's something that you're not telling me, and it's deeper than the pain of the unknown when it comes to Ty. Talk to me. It's what I'm here for."

My eyes stayed locked on the screen a few feet away as I tried to ignore the feelings that her keen observation had stirred up. When she put her fingers on my chin and turned my head to face her, I didn't resist. I actually allowed myself to fall into her brown bedroom eyes.

"Talk to me," she whispered seductively.

The deep breath that I took was a shuddering one that made my lungs feel like the wind was blowing around my chest cavity. It didn't make the words any easier to speak, but part of me knew that I needed to verbalize what had happened in order to start the grieving process.

"T-Tonya was pregnant... And the baby was mine. They killed my baby, and that shit is killing me inside because the only person who understands is God knows where."

I expected to see judgement of some sort dive into the pools of Carrie's eyes, but instead the only thing that I saw was compassion and understanding.

"I'm so sorry, David," she said, pulling me into her arms.

My body was stiff at first, but eventually, I melted into her and just let the sobs of heart aching pain fall from my mouth. Once the flood gates were open, I was utterly helpless to close them, so I gave myself over to the crying and just let it happen. Carrie didn't say a word. She simply held me tight and let me be vulnerable without fear or apology. I didn't know how long it lasted, but eventually, I was able to pull myself together and ease out of her embrace. The embarrassment that I felt was instantaneous but also unavoidable because I wasn't used to being vulnerable, and I never cried in front of people.

"Carrie, I uh..."

"You don't need to explain or be embarrassed, David. It takes a real man to be able to cry in front of a woman, and I respect you more for allowing me to be with you right now."

"I feel like I should thank you or something," I said, chuckling self-consciously.

"You don't gotta thank me, but I will ask you to trust me."

"Trust you? I think that I just demonstrated more trust in you than anyone at the moment by telling you a secret that would destroy my marriage," I replied.

"Believe me, David, every marriage has secrets, but do you wanna know what the trick is to keeping them? Trusting the person that you share them with."

She followed her statement with an unexpected action of standing up and offering me her hand. I was confused, but something about the twinkle in her eyes suggested that I take her hand, and so I did. I dropped the game controller as she pulled me to my feet, and I obediently followed her down the hallway to her bedroom. I hadn't been in here once since we'd arrived because the couch was my first and only conceivable option, but the sight of her plush, king-sized bed immediately had all types of thoughts racing through my mind.

"Carrie?" I said, pulling her to a stop just inside her bedroom doorway.

She stepped straight into my chest and looked up into my eyes with unashamed hunger.

"The rules are simple, David. No talking, unless it's nasty, no thinking, and no regrets. I want you to use my body in any way that you desire but only if you promise not to hold back."

I didn't know what to say and thinking damn sure wasn't happening fast enough for me to make it make sense. When she started to back away from me, I wanted to reach out and stop her, but a little voice whispered in my brain, telling me to wait. When she was standing beside the bed, she kicked off her Jordans and then pulled her T-shirt off over her head. Her jeans came off next, leaving her standing there in nothing except for a matching black bra with lace panties. My eyes stayed locked on hers as she moved with deliberate slowness that was effortlessly sexy when it came to unhooking her bra and letting it slide down her arm. The little wiggle that she did when pushing her panties down and stepping out of them put a smile on my face, but still we maintained heated eye contact. Lastly, she pulled her glasses off while taking her long brown hair out of its ponytail and added those accessories to the pile of clothing laying at her suckable toes. It was the breathtaking smile that made the temptation irresistible though, and I finally let my eyes roam down over her firm titties, farther south over her flat stomach, in between her thick thighs with her neatly trimmed pussy hair, and back up. The night that she'd got me out of jail was the first time I'd noticed her beauty and her booty, and now, they were mine for the taking. My secret was that I'd never slept with a white girl though, so I was curious and cautious too. The choice should've been easy, but it wasn't. It was the definition of complicated, and my mind flashed back to Shaomi. The last time I'd thought with my dick, shit had gone wrong in a karmic way. Even knowing that, I still began to undress until I stood as naked as she was, and then, I was moving toward her. Before I could grab her, she held up her hand, stopping my advance.

"Do you promise?" she asked seductively.

"Promise what?"

"Not to hold back," she replied, smiling mischievously.

My left band shot out swiftly, wrapping my fingers around her delicate neck as I pulled her to me hard and fast. Her gasp of surprise was caught in her throat because my mouth descended on hers with urgency and purpose. I wasn't just hungry. I was famished, and she'd just offered herself up as tribute to sate the animal in me.

Her tongue went to war with mine in a sweet dual, giving and taking, rolling and folding around mine like an experienced wrestler. When I felt her hand wrap around my dick, I bit her lip, which pulled a growl from her throat that sent tingles throughout my body. I broke the kiss but didn't let go of her neck as I spun her around. Instinctively, she widened her stance and leaned forward a little, and I wasted no time slipping my dick in between her pussy lips to find her heated ocean. I made sure to add force behind my strokes so that she was riding the balls of her feet for balance. With each stroke, my grip tightened on her throat and then relaxed, causing her pussy to mimic the action like we were holding the ropes playing double dutch. She made it hard to breathe because her pussy was tighter than a cock ring, but the way it felt made me say to hell with breathing. The strangled moans escaping her mouth worked like a shot of adrenaline, making me fuck her like I loved her. The moment that I felt like I was going to cum, I pulled my dick all the way out of her and bent her fully over the bed. Without hesitation, she braced with her arms out and tooted her big, pretty ass up at me like she was challenging me to tame her. With one hand on her hip, I grabbed my dick with the other and eased it in between her ass cheeks until I was knocking at my destination. Once I'd worked the head in, I grabbed her other hip and pulled her toward me while pushing forcefully inside her.

I felt the wind leave her body, but her grunt was one of satisfaction and pleasure that was punctuated by her throwing her ass back at me. With my second stroke, she'd adjusted to taking my full length in her asshole, and the fight began in a different arena. The battle of wills was the best that I could ever remember, but the moment that her arms gave out, and she collapsed on her neck, I smelled victory. My left leg went up on the bed as I switched holes again, diving back inside her tight pussy like I was trying to drive a tank through a little house. In that position, I pushed us to the brink, only to slow down and let the rebuild begin again. I waited until we were damn near exhausted before I finally rolled her onto her back and eased my dick inside her throbbing pussy that way.

"Look at me," she demanded breathlessly, putting her hand on my cheek.

I complied with her request, and we stayed just like that, fucking slow and steady until we both came in a duet of shaking and panting. Afterwards, it took a couple minutes for her pussy grip to loosen up enough for me to stop experiencing the aftershocks that had my dick still dripping inside her. I collapsed beside her, but I didn't even entertain the thought of sleeping. My mind actually drifted away from the great sex and began attacking the problems in my life from a different view. One universal truth about life was that it didn't matter how many people you killed. It only mattered who you killed.

"Glad that I could help," she said suddenly.

"Huh?" I asked, confused as I looked over at her.

I hadn't noticed her watching me, but the smile on her face signaled just that.

"That look in your eyes, that sheer focus. THAT'S the David that we all need to see, and if what just happened here could put that look back in your eyes, then you're welcome," she said, smiling widely.

I chuckled and pulled her toward me so that her head was laying on my chest. We didn't speak anymore, but that was okay because no words were needed. It was time to kill.

Chapter 10

(Royal)

(International Waters Between Miami and Cuba)

There was something about the calm lull of the ocean that comforted me as much as the chaos of a good storm excited me. For that reason, I'd purchased an eighty-foot yacht a couple years back, naming it BLUE BLOOD in dedication to my mother. One thing that no one could deny was that Sapphire, a.k.a. Jewel Sky, had been the mother who defined calm and chaos. So, naming my boat after her had seemed fitting. I kept a small crew of four on standby to work on the yacht, and when it wasn't in use, I kept it moored in Russia. Thanks to Kamile and Angel, our family had deep ties in Russia now, and I'd even met the president a couple of times. For my family, Russia was our version of Mexico, meaning a safe place to run from the laws of the United States and still be with the shit. It gave me pleasure to be able to introduce Tesha to these parts of my life, and as soon as we boarded the yacht, I noticed how she visibly relaxed. The constant movement of the ocean took some getting used to, especially with her still battling occasional morning sickness, but she'd adjusted. I made sure to have a nurse who qualified as a midwife on board too because I wanted to make sure Tesha and the baby were in perfect health. It still struck me as funny sometimes how quickly my mind and heart adjusted to being a father, almost husband, and protector, but I was my daddy's son, so that shit was in me, not on me. My life experiences made me wise beyond my years, so I felt no pressure about the roles that I'd assumed. I felt honored, and for the first time, I truly understood why my own dad moved certain ways when it came to protecting his family. Part of me wanted to call him and get his advice, but it wasn't time for that because I knew once I made that call, FatherGod would scorch the earth by fire. The same went for my sisters, although I doubted that I could keep them in the dark for long because I'd already missed three calls from them in the last week. They all wanted to meet the girl that they said kidnapped me with the pussy, which made me and Tesha laugh when I showed her their texts. I had no doubt that they would love her, but I didn't care if they didn't because when I looked at Tesha, I saw the possibility of forever. Just like right now.

"You trying to sneak up on me?" I asked, smiling as I turned around from the railing I'd been standing at, watching the ocean.

"I thought I was moving silently, but you must have eyes in the back of your head," Tesha replied, stepping into my open arms.

I pulled her to me and rested my chin on the top of her head while inhaling her familiar scent of peaches and vanilla. We stood there, entwined, not speaking as the colors of daylight came alive around us, transforming dusky purple into sun kissed orange.

"I could do this every day for all my days," she said, looking up into my eyes.

"If that's what you want, all you have to do is say the word, and it's done."

"Is it that simple?" she asked, smiling brightly.

"Do you suddenly doubt me now, sweetheart?"

"No, not in the slightest... But you can admit that we went from sexting and FaceTiming to being damn near married overnight. I've got no complaints at all. I just don't want us to burn out fast because we rushed everything," she replied.

"We haven't rushed EVERYHING," I said, giving her a mischievous smile.

She hit me playfully in the chest and laughed because we both found it funny that we still hadn't done anything physically sexual together yet. It wasn't because there was a lack of attraction in either of our parts. We both just agreed to let it happen naturally so that there was no pressure.

"I get your point, bae, but I promise that won't happen because we'll both keep our relationship spicy. I consider us to be partners, which means we both know how to compromise to make sure that our love keeps growing. That's a solid foundation to build on, so what else are you worried about?" I asked gently.

A look of guilt flashed in her hazel green eyes, followed by a look of embarrassment, but I didn't understand the source of either emotion that I was observing at war within her.

"Talk to me, Tesha. You know that I got you."

"Yeah, I know that you mean that when you say it, but what happens when the baby is born? What happens if David wants to be a part of her life?"

"Sweetheart, that little girl is innocent and a blessing that I hope everyone has the opportunity to enjoy. I'm not gonna stand in the way of David being a parent as long as he's respectful and he shows you the same respect as her mother and provider. If he can't or won't do that, then he's not welcome to be in her life because preserving her innocence at all costs is the goal," I replied sincerely.

"I'm worried about the fallout that'll take place between me and my sister if she ever finds out that her husband is my child's father."

"I understand that fear, but I feel like that's a lie to die with because the truth does nobody any good. On paper, it'll say that I'm her dad, and that's all anyone ever needs to know. Are you okay with that?" I asked.

"I love the idea of your name being on her birth certificate, but that will only happen under one condition that's nonnegotiable."

"Sounds serious. What is it?" I asked curiously.

"You have to name her."

The emotion of happiness that swelled up inside me was so unexpected that all I could do was smile and nod as I lowered my lips to hers. Our agreement was sealed with a gentle kiss that included a slow exploration of her mouth designed to turn her panties into a slip and slide. My hands ventured under the silk robe covering her curves so that I could rest my hands against her naked ass cheeks. The desire to lift her up and pin her to the yacht while fucking her was consuming every corner of my mind, but the feeling of being watched stopped me. I opened my eyes and reluctantly lifted my head away from hers in time to see one of the female crew members coming down from the upper deck.

"We're about to be interrupted, so why don't you go put some clothes on that sexy body while I put in our breakfast order?" I said.

"But a bitch is hungry for more than waffles and watermelon," she replied, squeezing my dick purposefully.

When she took a step back out of my arms and turned to walk away, it took everything in me not to follow behind her. What kept my feet rooted in place was the serious look in the eyes of the female approaching because it wasn't a look that came with good news.

"Mr. Walker, we have an incoming speed boat that looks to be on course for this vessel. How would you like to proceed?"

"Is it law enforcement?" I asked.

"It doesn't appear to be, but you better have a look for yourself, just to make sure."

I nodded and followed behind her while mentally considering the types of weapons that I had onboard the yacht. If someone came to fight me on water, then they were in for a long day because I had enough shit onboard for an invasion of Spain. By the time we made it to the upper deck, I could hear the faint echoes of a powerful engine bouncing off the waves to announce its presence. A pair of binoculars was passed my way, allowing me to scan the northwest horizon where I spotted the jet-black speed boat flying in our direction. The boat was as familiar as the passengers on it, and I wasn't surprised to see either. I was just more so trying to see around the unpredictability of what happened next.

"What do you wanna do, sir?"

"Nothing. Let the boat pull up and I'll handle it from there," I replied, passing the binoculars back to her and heading back downstairs.

I went straight to the master stateroom to find Tesha because she needed to be ready. My mistake was opening the door without knocking, and that was how I came to see her completely naked, lying on the bed, with two fingers working rhythmically inside her pussy. Even from the distance of a few feet away, I could still see the glistening juices running down the back of her knuckles, and I could hear the suction her fingers' motion was creating. Our eyes locked, and there was no shame or embarrassment anywhere in hers, which made her actions even sexier to me. The instant hardness of my dick was trying to drag me across the room to her, but the farthest that I got was stepping into her room and closing the door behind me. I couldn't find my voice to say a word, and the sound of her labored breathing was too erotic to interrupt regardless. I could see the green becoming more prominent in her eyes, accompanying the beautiful flush creeping up over her face. When she bit her lip and whined a little, I swore that I heard my knees knocking like big bass drums, threatening my ability to stand. I noticed the shaking in her legs too right before she opened them wider for me and started rubbing her clit vigorously. I felt my eyes bulge at the sight of her pretty pink pussy, but when her cum started to ooze out of her, my mouth dropped open. I could hear the speed boat clearly now, which meant that we had no time to finish what she'd started, but I silently vowed to myself that she was going to catch this fade as soon as possible.

"Did you-Did you enjoy the show?" she asked breathlessly, smiling wide as she sat up.

"I absolutely did, but we'll talk about that later. I need you to get dressed because we've got company."

"Company?" she asked.

In an instant, the sexy, coquettish look disappeared from her face and was replaced by fear.

"Yeah, my sisters are here."

For a split second, the look of fear morphed into panic, but just as quickly, she was able to reel it in and relax.

"Okay, I'll get dressed while you go find out what they want," she replied, licking her fingers as she stood up.

My mind got stuck on the fact that she'd just done the sexiest shit in the world by licking her own pussy juices off of her hand, but I shook it off and let myself out of the room. The whole way back upstairs, all I could see in my mind was what had just happened, and because of that, I could feel the smile spread across my face. By the time I got to the back of the yacht where the speed boat was being tied up, I'd convinced myself to get rid of my sisters as fast as possible because I had work to do.

"Does Dad know you're here?" I asked immediately.

"Well, hello to you too, little brother," Angel said, stepping aboard the yacht and hugging me.

Destiny and Free followed until we were all standing in a small circle.

"If Dad knew what you were out here in these streets doing, then he'd be breathing down your neck his damn self," Free stated, giving me that blank stare that signaled her annoyance.

"Dad knows that I came to see my girl," I replied defensively.

"But not that you stepped into the middle of a war," Destiny said knowingly.

The looks on my sisters' faces were almost identical, and they all told me that kicking them some bullshit would result in a fight. The beauty of the Walker sisters was undeniable by anyone with eyes, but I knew first-hand what their treachery looked like when you played with them. There was no way that I was about to do that again.

"Let's get a drink," I proposed facetiously, leading the way into the parlor just inside the back of the yacht.

"She's got you drinking liquor now?" Free asked from behind me.

"Always the mama bear, huh, Free?" I asked, chuckling as I took a seat on the white loveseat.

"Have you MET our sister?" Angel asked rhetorically.

Destiny and Free sat on the couch adjacent to me, and Angel plopped down in the plush chair across from me.

"So, it's obvious by your attire that you didn't come for the fun and sun part of my personal vacation. What's up?" I asked, ready to meet the bullshit head on.

"Don't get cute, Royal. You know exactly why we're here," Destiny replied.

"Honestly, I don't. I doubt that you came all this way to tell me to leave and stay out of this because you would know that I'm not doing either. So, I'm confused and curious as to the purpose of your visit since all questions and cussing could've been done over the phone," I said, smiling, much to my sisters' annoyance.

We may not have grown up together, but I most definitely knew how to be that little brother that made their nerves rub like two hands with some soap.

"Where is she?" Free asked with feigned patience and a smile that didn't quite reach the hazel in her eyes.

"I'm right here," Tesha said, breezing into the room wearing a rainbow-colored sundress and sitting down beside me.

No one spoke for a few moments, but the silent evaluations were louder than any argument I'd ever witnessed.

"Barefoot and pregnant looks good on you," Destiny said sarcastically.

"Thank you. I know," Tesha replied, smiling and reaching out to take my hand in hers.

"We need to know what you've gotten our little brother into besides what's in between your legs," Free said, obviously taking the not so delicate approach.

"It's funny that you mention that because he literally just saw my pussy before you interrupted, but he actually hasn't rode this ride yet. He insisted that we have this little sit down, but me personally, I would've rather been rocking this big boat," Tesha replied, still smiling sweetly.

My slight chuckle earned me deadly looks from my sisters, forcing me to clear my throat and swallow my smile.

"You sure that you wanna play with us, little girl?" Angel asked, smirking.

"Come at me serious and you'll get the same. Come at me with bullshit and I got that energy for you too," Tesha replied calmly.

The temperature in the room rose a few degrees, but it wasn't time to panic yet. I watched as Free moved with slow, deliberate motions, reaching behind her back and pulling out a Smith & Wesson wood grip, chrome 1911 .45 pistol that was clearly custom made.

"Royal, leave the room," Destiny demanded.

"Nah, I think I'll stay," I replied, gripping Tesha's hand tighter.

"It's okay, Royal. I got this. Leave," Tesha said.

I was more than hesitant already, and then Free pulled the slide on her pistol, which signaled the time for debating over with. Shit was more than real, and for the first time, I questioned what I'd gotten Tesha into.

Chapter 11

(Tynesha)

"Y-You're really gonna give me to Zoe Pound?" I asked, unable to keep the fear out of my voice any longer.

Roland didn't respond. He simply walked out of the bathroom and disappeared from my sight. I'd been doing my best to keep my emotions bottled up inside, but the impending doom had my panic level high enough to have tears pouring from my eyes. There was no doubt in my mind that Zoe Pound would kill me and my child, and they would enjoy every moment of anguish they could inflict along the way. It was the unknown torture that I would be forced to endure on this journey to death that I feared the most. I could only die once, but how I got there always terrified me. No type of mercy would be given, and begging would undoubtedly make it that much worse. That left me with only two options - embrace death or fight with everything I had in me to save mine and my child's life. That fight wasn't just a physical one though, which meant that I needed to think faster than I ever had before. The first thing that I had to do was force myself to calm down because I could feel the hysteria bubbling up around the panic, and that was the worst thing I could give into. For a full minute, all I kept repeating in my mind were the words, JUST BREATHE, and that helped me to slow my heart rate down somewhat. The sound of rapid gunfire being exchanged completely fucked up my meditation though, and the panic was right back on my chest like a fat bitch. My survival mind kicked in, and I was able to view whatever was happening outside as the necessary distraction that I needed.

I took stock of my situation swiftly, and then, I used all my weight to pull on the shower rod. After the fifth try, one side finally came down off the wall, and I was able to work my cuffed wrists off the pole. Immediately, I ran into the bedroom and hurriedly put on my panties and shorts, but there was no way to get my shirt and bra on. The feeling of vulnerability that came with running with my titties bouncing everywhere made me pause for a second, but I quickly said fuck it in the name of survival. Once my feet slid into my shoes, I took off toward the bedroom door. When I pulled it open, I could hear the gunfire loud and clear, and I silently prayed for its continuance because whoever was firing definitely had Roland's attention. When I made it to the top of the steps, I could literally see the bullets flying through the wood of the front door, turning it into splinters and dust. The gamble that I was taking was obvious, but there was no other way to get downstairs and outside. I crept down the stairs slowly, trying to time my next move like I was a girl again jumping rope. As soon as I heard a break in the shots being fired from a distance due to Roland shooting back, I flew down the steps. I saw Roland on my left out of my peripheral vision, which instinctively made me go right and run toward the back of the house that way.

"Ty!" Roland yelled.

I ignored him and kept running like my shoes had jet packs in them, weaving around furniture as my eyes locked on the back door leading outside. I ran as fast as my legs would carry me, feeling more motivated by the fact that I could hear Roland coming after me. When I got to the door, I snatched it open and came face to face with a tall, brown skin man holding a .357 revolver with a huge smile on his face. I wasted no time with words, knowing that they would do me no good, and instead I dove away from the door. I heard the gun go off simultaneously with my movement, and then, I felt the heat accompanied by the blinding pain from the shot that hit my shoulder. It felt like the wind had been kicked out of me, making it impossible for me to scream or cry out. The sound of bullets flying from behind me and over my head resulted in the nigga who'd shot me dropping to his knees and his smile transforming into death's blank stare. My mind was screaming at me to get the fuck back up and keep moving, but before I could put thought to action, Roland grabbed me by a fistful of my hair.

"You trying to get your silly ass shot? If not, then do what the fuck I tell you and don't think about running outside again," he demanded, dragging me back toward the front of the house.

I was forced to follow him because he still had a firm grip on my hair, but everything in me was silently swearing to get him back for this shit someday. Before we got back to the stairs, he stopped at a door that opened on a small closet and tossed me inside.

"Stay put," he said, like I was some type of bad dog.

The only feeling that I knew in this moment was hatred, and it was radiating from my heart and soul. The pain of landing up against a wall and banging my fast-bleeding shoulder took my focus away from Roland but only for the briefest second. I was quickly plunged into darkness when Roland shut the door on me, and I heard the sound of scraping wood as a piece of furniture banged up against the door. I had no idea what Roland's plan was, but it wasn't lost on me that he had saved my life for whatever reason. I still hated his bitch ass, but I could at least see the sense in waiting where I was to see who lived and who died. I'd hoped that whoever was shooting at Roland was part of a rescue attempt for me, and even though I didn't know for sure, it didn't feel like that. It could've been me judging the man at the back door by his dreadlocks, but this felt like the Haitians had descended on us. I could still hear shots ringing out, but there weren't as many guns being fired. I had no idea how long I sat there in the dark, holding my stomach and praying, before I realized that even the sporadic gunfire had stopped. Anybody else would've probably felt some type of relief, but I didn't. The fear only intensified because I knew that no matter who survived, it was still going to be torture on the menu for me. That knowledge made me want to get up and take a run at the door, and the only reason that I didn't was because of the sudden fatigue that came over me. I was losing too much blood, and I was helpless to stop it. I crawled to my feet, refusing to go down without continuing to fight as I stumbled in the direction of the door. I used my right hand to steady myself against the door, and then, I placed my right shoulder on it so that I could push without screaming in pain. Before I could get my feet set though, I heard the familiar sound of wood scraping, and then, the door was pulled open by none other than Roland himself.

"I guess that you're the lesser of two evils," I mumbled, collapsing into his arms.

If he responded, I didn't hear it because I was losing consciousness. When I came to, it was only long enough to realize that I was stretched across the backseat of an SUV, wrapped in a blanket, and then, I was gone again. It felt like I was dreaming because I kept seeing images of my mom, my twin, and my husband in a colorful kaleidoscope kind of way. I didn't feel the comfort that one would expect to feel over nostalgic feelings of loved ones though. I only felt... cold. As physical as the feeling was, it still felt like it resonated from somewhere deep within my soul. Before I had the presence of mind to analyze my feelings further, I was snatched back into consciousness by excruciating pain in my shoulder. It only took a few seconds to realize that the man looming over me in an opened collared shirt with his tie loosened was the source intensifying my pain because he was fucking with my shoulder.

"Roland!" I gasped in pain.

"Stop moving, Ty. He trying to get the bullet out," Roland replied.

I couldn't see him, but I could definitely see the metal clamps that were already inside my shoulder. My only chance at sanity was to avert my head and growl through the pain without moving too much. It seemed like forever before the bullet was finally pulled out of me, and the relief that I felt almost made me pass back out.

"She gonna make it, Doc?" Roland asked.

"It's too early to tell because she's lost a lot of blood. Let me sew her up and then we'll talk."

I was too exhausted to be worried by the uncertainty of my prognosis, and nothing that I could think about kept my heavy eyelids form closing, so I gave up the fight. This time, unconsciousness didn't bring visions of my family, but instead, it was me holding my daughter in my arms. Her smile looked like twenty percent mine and eighty percent David's, but it was so much more than beautiful, and it eased the coldness that had been lingering within me. It felt like hours that I spent just holding our little angel, but when I opened my eyes again, the white doctor was still sewing the hole in my shoulder closed. I could see Roland behind him, pacing the floor anxiously, with a gun in his hand.

"Help," I whispered, locking eyes with the doctor and praying he could see my distress for what it really was.

The fact that Roland didn't stop pacing or break stride told me that he hadn't heard my plea, but I could tell that the doctor had. I could see confusion in his blue eyes, causing me to shhh him before he could ask a question that would get us both killed. I knew that he didn't understand that I was a hostage because Roland had been smart enough to remove the handcuffs from my wrists at some point. I had no idea what this man's relationship was to Roland, but I knew that I might never get this chance again.

"David Bishop," I whispered quickly, barely moving my lips.

"What did she say?" Roland asked, suddenly popping up over the doctor's right shoulder.

"I don't know. The pain has probably made her delirious by now. Do you want me to give her some oxy?" the doctor asked, giving me a wink that only I could see.

"She can't take that when she's pregnant. Do you have anything else?" Roland asked.

"Sure. Grab my medical bag off the bookcase over there."

The moment that Roland disappeared, the doctor turned his undivided attention back to me.

"Find David. Find my husband."

The doctor nodded as he slipped what appeared to be a scalpel into my shorts pocket. The relief that flooded my bloodstream was only overpowered by one thing. Hope.

Chapter 12

(David)
(Plant City, Florida)

The quiet of the streets on the late nights spoke to me and made me feel one with the shadows as we rolled into town. Plant City, Florida was a spot that few people actually knew about in terms of the dirt under its fingernails, but I was one of the few with inside knowledge. I knew hustlers, hoes, and killers that walked these streets, and they were indistinguishable from the blue-collar workers who clocked a normal nine to five job. The person I was looking for tonight was a chameleon of sorts and the perfect jack-of-all-trades that was needed for my next move. I'd met Kelvin years ago when he blew through Orlando, trying to outrun the U.S. Marshalls that had tracked him from Virginia on a fugitive warrant. A friend of a friend had vouched for him, so I'd tossed him a half a pound of some good gas, and the next thing I knew, he was riding around town in a black Rolls Royce Phantom. The streets called him Squirrel, and it made sense because the nigga only needed a little to survive while he stored the rest away. He'd had a good run in Florida, but eventually, the warrant he had in Williamsburg, Virginia couldn't be avoided, so he was forced to go home. I made sure to keep in touch because that was what real niggas did, and once he was back in the streets, he came straight back to Florida. Prison had furthered his education too because now he knew about scamming, which was faster money for lower risk. Most niggas believed in the out of sight out of mind philosophy when it came to scamming, but the nigga, Squirrel, moved differently, and that was what made his skill set more valuable. By day, he lived like the one percent of rich people because he had that bag to do so due to saving and investing in the right things. By night, he roamed the streets like a panhandler begging for change and essentially becoming invisible because people tended to ignore the homeless. He saw and heard shit that people wanted kept secret, and it put him in a rare position of having a vault of information that would aid my next move.

"Are you sure he's out here?" Carrie asked again.

"I'm sure," I replied, keeping my eyes peeled for his familiar stocky frame.

We'd been riding around for half an hour, but I was committed to stay out as long as it took for me to bump into this nigga accidentally on purpose. If Carrie kept asking questions though, I was going to drop her ass off at a hotel or something. I didn't verbalize my thoughts because I knew that her only intention was to be helpful in this situation, and she was all I had to lean on right now. I might not have been able to admit it to her, but deep down, I knew that I absolutely needed her more than I'd previously realized.

"We're out of blunt wraps," she said, looking up from her purse.

"There's a 7-Eleven right there. We can stop real quick."

I guided the SUV to a stop in front of the store, and before I could offer to go inside, she'd hopped out of the truck and sauntered toward the door.

For a few moments, I watched the sway of her hips in her low rider jeans, admiring the beat of her drums that was effortlessly full of sensual seduction. The dopest part about Carrie was that she was one of those bad bitches who didn't even know how bad she really was. It wasn't just the crazy body, her beauty, humor, or intelligence. It was the combination and how well that shit meshed together that made her the star of any team. This was probably why her husband put a ring on it, but she was still too much of a wild and free spirit to be tamed by vows. She was definitely special though, and as I continued watching her, I saw a nigga step out of the shadows to admire the same beauty that I was. I immediately recognized Squirrel's brown skin, 5'6, two hundred twenty-five pound frame even though he had grown some short dreadlocks since the last time I'd seen him. The look of hunger when it came to women hadn't changed though, and if I would've thought about that sooner, I could've had Carrie leading the search party long ago. I watched in amusement as Squirrel attempted to dust himself off and smooth his hair up into a quick man bun, trying to make himself look like anything but a bum ass nigga in this moment. The part that made me laugh out loud was when he gave himself the smell check by lifting his armpit toward his face because his wince was visible, even in the darkness. He shrugged that shit off like it was an unimportant factor though and proceeded to post up outside the store where Carrie was guaranteed to cross his path. Part of me wanted to get out of the truck and stop this train wreck, but the petty nigga in me just kept watching. A few seconds later, Carrie reappeared with a Slurpee in one hand, headed back toward me. I couldn't hear the exchange, but it was obvious by his body language that Squirrel was kicking flav at Carrie, and she was trying to politely ignore him. I saw the shift in her eyes though when he took a step toward her, and I knew the time for sniggling and giggling was over. The door was open, and my feet were on the ground immediately, and the first thing I heard was Carrie's voice telling him that she was married.

"Yo, Squirrel," I said, coming around the front of the SUV just as he was opening his mouth to respond to her.

Recognition dawned clear and instant in his dark brown eyes, and I saw him reevaluate the entire situation in a split second.

"Damn, nigga, where the fuck did you come from?" he asked, laughing.

"Shit, I'm out here looking for you," I replied.

"Oh, so you put this white girl bait in the water on purpose? You always was a smart muthafucka," he said, laughing again as he came toward me and dapped me up.

As we half hugged, I gave Carrie a slight nod that told her to get back in the truck, leaving me and him alone for the moment.

"I've been hearing your name a lot out here in these streets, so I'm surprised to see you out here. This must be important," he said, looking at me squarely.

"Money is always an important thing, my nigga."

"Yeah, it is, but in this case, I'mma need to know what's attached to this money and if it outweighs the bounty that Zoe Pound put on your head," he replied honestly.

"Fair enough. Take a ride with me," I said, leading him to the backseat of Carrie's SUV as I signaled for her to get in the driver's seat.

I slid in behind Squirrel, but I didn't speak again until we had pulled off.

"How big is the bounty?" I asked.

"100K, dead or alive, and the preference is dead. The same goes for everyone in your family and anyone associated with you. Shit, just being seen with you can get a nigga's top popped," he replied.

"I need to know where Zoe Pound is hiding Roland because he has my wife, and she's pregnant with my baby. I also need your help getting to Councilman Viktor Bah because he's the head of this particular snake, and I intend to sever that head."

"Well, I'll give you some free info first and some great advice second. Zoe Pound ain't hiding Roland. They're hunting that nigga, and if he kidnapped your wife, then she's as dead as he is when they catch him. More importantly though, Councilman Bah is one of many heads on this hydra you're tangling with, and I advise you to let that go. You grabbed the snake by the tail, and now it's pissed off. I know you ain't no bitch, bruh, but running is your only sane option because Bah is head hunting after what you did to his wife and daughter," he said.

"I didn't do shit to that man's peoples because I was laid up in the hospital where his bitch ass put me!"

"It don't matter if you were the one who tortured and killed them or if you were just the one who hung them from the freeway overpass. It was done on your order. It was a statement, and that statement can only be atoned for with more blood," he replied calmly.

The truth of his words put a bad taste in my mouth, but I wasn't the fool to argue against the sense he was making. I knew that me and mine were up to our necks in this shit, so the options were either swim or drown.

"If what you're saying is true, then you know that running ain't an option, especially because that's what these niggas expect me to do. I gotta go against the grain, so the only question is are you down to help me?" I asked.

"Nah, this ain't my fight... but I'll help myself if the price is right," he replied, smiling.

I hadn't expected any less from the man sitting to my left, but I caught the look of disgust on Carrie's face through her reflection in the rearview mirror.

"250K right now," I offered, pulling my phone out.

"Sounds like we've got an understanding," he replied readily.

It took us about ten minutes to move money from one of my secret accounts into one of his choosing and for the verification to be confirmed. While that was being done, Carrie had pulled over on a dark residential street and rolled a blunt that she lit and passed to me in the backseat. I smoked slowly while I listened to Squirrel tell me about Councilman Bah's main mistress, Marta, that he kept hidden in Ft. Lauderdale. Her and her son, Paco, lived in a nice house that was bought through one of the councilman's shell companies, Litework LLC, and the only reason that Squirrel knew this was because he'd accidentally tried to liquidate that company's assets.

Once he'd found out who he tried to rob, he saw the benefit in playing the long game because it was obvious to him that the councilman was more that crooked. He was straight up twisted.

"Are you sure Bah is down there now?" Carrie asked, accepting the blunt when I passed it to her.

"I mean, I ain't been down there to cut the nigga's grass or nothing, but based on my intel, I know that he turned that house into his base of operations after he got shot. That muthafucka is supposedly a fortress too because the mistress is connected to some serious people her damn self. Bah got himself a sexy Latina that's with the shit, so you know what that means," he replied, looking over at me.

"Yeah, that means that she's his weakness that can be exploited," I stated, thinking about the women in my life that I'd bury a nigga for fucking with.

The look that Carrie gave me through the rearview mirror told me that she was reading my mind, which she confirmed with a wink.

"I'm gonna tell you like this though, David. If you do this, you better go scorched Earth biblical with it. You can't afford to miss so aim true, my nigga," he advised.

"I hear you... So, let me ask you a question. If it was you, how would you hit Bah?"

Squirrel contemplated the question for a moment in silence before giving a decisive nod that signaled his inner voice coming to a conclusion of some sort.

"I'd hit him simultaneously, but in order for that to work, you'd either have to be in two places at once or have help. Like I told you from the jump, this ain't my fight though."

"What would the second target be?" Carrie asked.

"There's the port in Miami because that's the center of Zoe Pound's criminal enterprise. Everything comes in through the port, including people, so finding a way to control that affects his power in a major way. If you can't feed your wolves, then they'll put your ass on the menu," he replied.

An idea popped into my head instantly, but I knew that there was no way to pull it off with just Carrie by my side. I was going to have to swallow my pride, and maybe if I'd done that sooner, then Tonya and our baby would be alive.

"Is there somewhere we can drop you off?" I asked, making it clear that our business was concluded for the moment.

"Nah, my nigga, you know that I'm an expert at finding my own way. I hope to see you again soon though. Miss Lady, you take care of that sexy ass body, baby," he replied, blowing a kiss at Carrie as he got out of the SUV.

"Ugh!" she exclaimed once the door was closed.

I chuckled as she wasted no time pulling off, like she was trying to outrun someone giving chase.

"You've got some wonderful friends, David," she said sarcastically.

"Useful, I think, is the word you're looking for."

"Whatever. What's our next move?" she asked.

"We need reinforcements, and we need them fast because we gotta knock the wind out of Zoe Pound before they catch up to Roland and Ty. Head to Miami while I make a call that I'd vowed never to make."

Chapter 13

(Royal)

"I'm staying. End of discussion," I said, squeezing Tesha's hand to quiet her objections while keeping my focus on Free.

The gun in my big sister's hand didn't scare me for real because I'd seen her get with the shit, but the look in her eyes was the cause for concern. She was in full protective mode, and that made anyone expendable who wasn't family.

"We're not here to play with you, and you need to know that. Now, explain to us what our tender dick little brother has put himself in the middle of," Free demanded, speaking in a deadly calm voice that I knew so well.

This time, it was Tesha who squeezed my hand to keep me from saying anything. I had no idea what she intended to say to my extremely unreasonable siblings, but I felt like I had to trust her and have her back.

"Listen, I understand why you all are so protective when it comes to Royal and your family as a whole. I respect it because I live by the same principles, especially when it comes to my twin, Tynesha. This fight wasn't mine, but if you come for mine, then I'm in it regardless. If you can understand that then there's room for a real conversation, but if you came just to try and scare me away from Royal then you're wasting your time," Tesha said passionately.

Destiny and Angel looked at each other, but Free kept her eyes locked on Tesha. I recognized the look of a predator evaluating the options before making any move because they understood the domino effect. After a few moments, Free gave a subtle nod, and I instantly felt Tesha's hand relax in mine. That was the only outward sign that she'd been any type of nervous, and when she began talking, her tone was possessed with confidence. The rest of us sat in silence as Tesha rewound time with her explanation of how things had gone so horribly wrong. She talked about her working with the nigga, Roland, his obsession, and their retaliation against Zoe Pound, but she kept the fact that her twin's husband was her baby daddy to herself. I silently agreed with this by giving her hand a light squeeze. Neither of us needed the judgement that was sure to come with that revelation. It took almost half an hour for Tesha to get the whole story out, and by the time she was done, I could feel the emotional exhaustion rolling off of her.

Without hesitation, I pulled her toward me and wrapped my arm around her so that she could rest her head on my shoulder. Free looked over at Angel and Destiny, which I knew meant that they could speak first while she continued to process what she'd heard.

"Royal, what do you think about all of this?" Angel asked.

"From a strategic standpoint, I know that I can outthink and out maneuver these Zoe Pound niggas, but it's harder to fight the opps when I've got to keep one eye on Tesha," I replied honestly.

"Okay, so if that wasn't an issue, do you think you can handle this?" Destiny asked.

"You know I can, so what's the real question that you all wanna ask me? Give it to me straight with no chaser," I said.

"Do you need our help, or do you need us to call Dad?" Free asked pointedly.

It was on the tip of my tongue to say that I didn't give a fuck if she called Dad, but I knew that she'd do that on general principle if I said that smartass shit. So, I swallowed those words and prepared to say something different, but I was saved by my ringing phone. I pulled it out of my pocket like it was on fire, and even though I didn't recognize the number of the incoming call, I still answered the call.

"Yeah?" I said.

"It's David. We need to talk."

The surprise that I felt right now was only able to be suppressed by me standing up and going outside to the back of the yacht. After a quick reminder to myself not to pop off on this nigga, I was mentally prepared for whatever bullshit he was kicking.

"What's up, David?"

"I got a plan, but I need your help. How quick can you get to Miami?" he asked.

"It won't take long. What's the move?"

"First, we cripple Zoe Pound's infrastructure, and then, we go after my wife. Roland has her, but Zoe Pound wants his head too, so I'm sure that he's gonna be running scared with his pussy ass. With them neutralized, he should be easier to hunt and find," David replied.

"I like what I'm hearing. Where do you wanna link up?"

"Call this number when you're in the city and we'll pick a spot," he replied.

"I'm on the way," I said, hanging up and stepping back into the parlor.

All eyes were on me immediately, but I just went back to my seat beside Tesha and reclaimed my position.

"To answer your question, Freedom, if I need help, you know that I'll call you, so there's no reason to bring Dad into this. Him, Madeline, and Truth are living their best lives, and we owe it to them to allow some normalcy into this family for once," I said.

"We don't do normal," Destiny said.

"And we don't keep secrets," Angel chimed in.

"Lil nigga, did you use my government name though?" Free asked, gripping her pistol in her hand a little tighter.

"Let him live, Free. You know that he was just trying to distract us from asking about the obviously important call that he had to take outside," Destiny said.

I opened my mouth to say the word MUTHAFUCKA, but it never passed my lips before Angel started chuckling.

"You thought that you got away with that weak shit, baby brother?" Angel asked, shaking her head sadly.

"Who was it, bae? Tesha asked, looking up at me.

For the moment, I ignored my sisters and focused on the woman who made my heart beat faster because I owed her the truth.

"It was David. He said that he has a plan to hurt Zoe Pound's infrastructure which will open the door to finding Tynesha."

"Does he know if Tynesha is still alive?" Free asked.

"I don't know. All he said was that the nigga who kidnapped her ain't protected by Zoe Pound anymore, so once we get them out of the way, it should be pretty easy to find him," I replied.

"That makes sense," Destiny said.

"When and where do you put the plan into play?" Tesha asked.

"As soon as I get back to Miami, but..."

My voice trailed off because I didn't know how to walk away from Tesha, even if I was sending her to safety. In my heart, I felt like I was the only one who could really keep her safe, and I wouldn't forgive myself if something happened to her or the baby.

"Royal, we'll take care of Tesha," Angel said, reading my hesitation clearly.

"You don't have to do that. I can find somewhere safe for her to lay low," I replied.

"We know that we don't HAVE to do it, but it's what family does. You've said through words and actions that Tesha and the baby are your family now, so we stand behind her like we do you," Free said sincerely.

"Anything you need other than that, we got you. All you gotta do is say the word," Destiny said.

The emotion that I felt was overwhelming and completely uncharacteristic, so I kept my mouth shut for a moment to gather my thoughts. The love that I saw in Tesha's eyes put a lump in my throat, but she soothed the thunder and lightning inside me by placing her hand over my heart and giving me a gentle kiss. Moments like this made me forget that I was a gangsta, but I enjoyed it nonetheless until I heard one of my sisters clearing her throat purposefully.

"Your little puppy love is cute, but there's work to be done, bruh," Angel said.

"That's the same shit that we used to try and tell you when you and Lil Boy first got together," Destiny said, laughing.

"Nobody asked you for your opinion, Baby Dee, so shut up," Angel replied, pushing her playfully.

"Are they always like this?" Tesha whispered to me.

"Mmm hmm. Thicker than thieves and loyal to a fault, but that's why I love them and trust them with you. You'll be safe with them," I assured her.

She didn't question. She just nodded and gave me another quick kiss.

"Destiny, go tell the crew and captain that we set sail for Russia within the hour. Angel, I want you to check in wit Dad and tell him that we decided to take a little vacation that's putting us in his neck of the woods," Free instructed.

"What are you gonna tell Dad?" I asked apprehensively.

"The truth - or at least most of it. I'm not bout to get shot for lying to that nigga but don't worry because I'll make sure that he knows the situation is under control. Madeline will keep him on the sideline and out of the game, but now you know that you'll have the full weight of the family behind you should the need arise," Free replied.

"Thanks, sis," I said.

"It's what family does, fool. Now, you need to take the speed boat and go handle the business so that I don't gotta look at the sad expression on your girl's face for too long. You know that I don't do that mushy shit. We'll keep the yacht close to the shore and pick you up when you call," Free said.

I laughed even though I could see Tesha blushing out of the corner of my eye.

"Your ass is soft now, Free, and you have been for the last few years," I replied, standing up and taking Tesha's hand to pull her to her feet.

"Try me and see if I don't fuck you up," Free said, smiling devilishly.

I waved her comment off as I led Tesha outside and down to the speed boat. I could feel her tense up with every step, and I knew that this brief separation was going to hit a little different for both of us because we'd been glued at the hip since I landed.

"This shouldn't take long, bae, so try not to stress and focus on our beautiful little girl that will arrive before you know it. I want you to start mentally making a home for us, and you get to pick any place in the world to go."

"I don't care where we are as long as we're together," she replied, reaching up to wrap her arms around my neck.

"That sounds good to me as long as you never expect a normal life because my sister, Destiny, already told you that we don't do that."

"Like that's really a change for me," she said, laughing softly.

To me, it felt dangerous to have a long, drawn-out goodbye because that signaled that I wasn't coming back, and I wasn't about to speak that into existence.

"Let's keep this short and sweet. I love you, and I'll see you in a minute," I said, kissing her on the forehead.

"I love you too, but you're not leaving without naming our daughter."

The fact that her arms tightened around my neck told me that she was so serious, but that only made me smile as I put my hand against her stomach.

"Her name, huh? Well... I'll give her two names, and you pick the middle. How bout that?" I asked.

"No deal, bae. You name her because you saved her. End of discussion."

Her stubbornness was cute, and I instinctively kissed the tip of her nose.

"Fine. Our daughter's name will be Stormy Blue Walker," I declared, looking down into her eyes.

"Sounds perfect. I love you, and the sooner that you get back, the sooner I can show you in more ways than ever before," she said, kissing me as her hand quickly slipped inside my shorts.

Before I could breathe, she had a firm grip on my dick that left me speechless.

Her lips smacked against mine loudly, and then she was out of my arms, sauntering back inside while giggling at my expense because I was stuck like a fork in the road. I did my best to gather my composure and focus, but all I could see in my mind's eye was making love to her over and over again. These thoughts accompanied me aboard the speed boat and carried me the forty-five minutes that it took for me to get back to the port of Miami. Once I hit dry land though, I pushed the sweet shit from my mind and focused on the task in front of me. Murder.

I called David, and he gave me directions to a hotel, so I grabbed a Lyft and headed in that direction. When I arrived at room 1012, the door was opened by a cute, thick, white girl with glasses and sexy brown eyes.

"You must be Royal."

"I am, and who are you?" I asked.

"I'm Carrie. Nice to meet you."

We shook hands in a formal way, but her hand lingered in mine a few seconds too long, and the blush that crept up over her face told me that she felt it too. When she sidestepped to allow me to enter the room, I saw David standing by a huge queen-sized bed full of weapons.

"Going to war?" I asked casually.

"Absolutely, but we're gonna need something a little bigger for what I have in mind."

"Well, you've definitely got my attention, so how can I help?" I asked.

"You can help by living up to the reputation of your family name because this shit is about to get ugly, and the only ones who need to survive are the ones on our team. Everybody else dies."

Chapter 14

(Tynesha)

"Is she gonna make it, Doc?" Roland asked again.

"She should, but she needs a lot of rest and a hospital in case a blood transfusion becomes necessary. The next forty-eight hours can be critical for her if she's not careful."

"You know that we can't go to the hospital because of the questions that they will ask," Roland replied with mounting frustration.

"Well, then, I guess your only option is to keep her here where I can monitor her for the next couple of days."

My eyes remained half closed so that I could continue listening to their conversation undetected, but I was definitely watching Roland's reaction to what the doctor was saying. His hesitation over what the doc was suggesting was clear, and his silence spoke to the indecision because he didn't want to make the wrong move for multiple reasons.

"Are you equipped to handle her condition should anything go wrong, William?" Roland asked.

If his use of the doctor's first name was meant to be intimidating or threatening, both goals were accomplished easily. I had no idea what history these two men shared, but it was clear that William had a good idea about who Roland was deep down.

"My home office in the back room is complete with a hospital bed, I.V., drip, heart and blood pressure monitors. I've got everything that you could find in a hospital room, and if we need to do a transfusion, then I can go to the hospital and get the blood myself. Do you know her blood type?"

"Yeah, its O negative," Roland replied casually.

The shock that I felt made me want to throw up, but I fought like hell to keep playing like I was two steps away from death. I didn't know how this nigga knew my blood type, but it was definitely creepy as fuck!

"Okay, then, I'll keep her here for a couple days, and you can notify her family in case they want to come and check on her here. I've got a friend that's a neonatal nurse, and she'll come to check on the baby if I call her."

"No, no one else needs to know that she's here. I'm the only family that she's got, and you can make sure the baby is alright yourself," Roland replied, slightly aggressive.

"Okay, I understand," William conceded quickly.

The tension in the room felt like it was breathing for the two men, and I knew that Roland would feed on it, so I offered up the timely distraction by moaning weakly. Instantly, Roland was at my side, kneeling next to me and stroking my hair gently enough to make the good doctor think that he actually cared about me. I felt the vomit at the base of my throat, slushing against my vocal cords like waves crashing against rocks on the shoreline, but I kept it from spraying upwards. It took all of my willpower though.

"Hey, sweetie. You're okay, just try not to move too fast or too much because those stitches are fresh," Roland warned.

"Where am I?" I asked.

"Don't worry. You're safe, and the baby is fine. Just rest," Roland replied, still gently stroking my hair.

He kept the loving and caring facade up until William walked out of the room for something, and then, he leaned down so that his lips were pressed right against my ear.

"Don't try any slick shit that's gonna get that man killed. He saved your life, and all you have to do to save his is act normal so that he doesn't suspect a thing. I'm gonna leave the handcuffs off of you, but I promise that the first time you fuck up, they go back on," he said.

Everything in me wanted to spit in this nigga's face with the same urgency and passion as when he had me strung up in the shower, but I knew that I was definitely too weak now to start this fight. I needed to continue to play shit smart. When he lifted his head away from my face and looked up, I could tell that he was looking for Dr. William, which I didn't need him to do because hopefully he was handling the mission for me.

"What happened back at the house?" I asked, taking his hand to keep him still.

"The double cross happened. You were right when you said that we should've left, but I really didn't think that they could find out about that house because it was paid for in cash by a third party."

"Did you shoot first?" I asked.

"Of course I did. I knew that they were there to kill me, which would get you and the baby killed too, so I went on the offensive."

I tried to stop myself from asking the next question, but as soon as my mouth opened, I knew that it was a lost cause.

"Weren't you about to offer me and the baby up to save your own ass?"

"No, I just said that to scare you and buy more time with them so that we could safely escape Florida undetected," he replied.

His explanation seemed plausible and more in line with the nigga I'd known him to be versus the piece of shit I thought he'd become. I still wasn't dumb enough to trust his ass though.

"So, what's the plan now?" I asked, hoping to keep him distracted a little while longer.

"Honestly, I don't know. I'm trying to keep you and our baby safe, but my resources are drying up thanks to Zoe

Pound putting a big price tag on my head. The fact that I know too much has made me public enemy number two in their eyes, and number one is David. I'm hoping that he can distract them for us so that we can leave the country."

"Leave the country? And go where with no passports?" I asked.

"That's a problem that we'll worry about later. Right now, I need you to rest up and gather your strength so that you can heal as quick as possible."

My emotions were conflicting with each other because, on the one hand, I appreciated Roland keeping me safe from niggas that wanted me dead with a passion, but his lack of a concrete plan scared me. This wasn't a situation where a muthafucka could simply hope for the best. You had to pray, and if necessary, you had to prey because niggas were serious when they said kill or be killed. I knew that Roland understood this because he'd been surrounded by it, but he was so used to having Zoe Pound as his security blanket that he didn't realize that he needed to be ten moves ahead of the opps.

"I know one place that we'll be safe, and we won't need passports to get into the country," I said, measuring my words carefully.

"Oh, really? And where might that be?"

The sarcasm in his voice was grating on my last nerve, but I pushed past the feelings of anger to finish setting my plan in motion.

"Africa. My cousin, Shaomi, is over there dating some prince or something, and I'm sure that he has the pull to get us into the country," I replied calmly.

He didn't respond immediately, but the look on his face gave away the fact that his brain was putting in some overtime in the thinking department.

"You wouldn't be trying to trick me?" he asked in a calm tone with deadly currents entwined in the question.

"Trick you? Trick you how, Roland? I'm just trying not to get us killed."

"That may be true, but the last time I saw your cousin, Shaomi, she was sky high due to the car bomb that was meant for your precious David. You're trying to tell me that she survived that?" he asked skeptically.

"That's exactly what I'm telling you, and after that, she fled the country. She doesn't know that you were behind the bombing, and you already know that she hasn't been around like that to know about me and you over the years. She'll figure that I'm just following her lead and trying to keep my baby safe."

"Our baby," he said, making sure to emphasize his point.

"Yes, our baby, Roland. The point is that we'll be safe and able to start over."

"I get the point, Tynesha, but in order for me to believe it, I'd need to hear it from Shaomi's mouth."

"That's fine. Give me your phone," I demanded.

His hesitation was immediate and obvious, but I knew that he'd realize just how boxed in he was if I just gave him a few seconds to run through the play on his own. I gave him the moment that he needed without interrupting him, knowing in the back of my mind that William being gone this long only meant good things for me.

"I'm telling you now that if you do something stupid, you'll regret it for many lives to come," he vowed, pulling his phone out of his pocket.

I rolled my eyes as I took it from his hand and mentally prepared to do the best acting job of my life.

"Just follow my lead," I instructed, glancing at him briefly.

He nodded, and I finished the process by hitting the send button. I had no idea what time it was in Africa, but I knew that it had to be daylight because the night sky was showing outside the windows of William's house. After a few seconds, Shaomi's face filled the screen, and I felt relief unlike anything I'd known since hearing that my baby was okay.

"Hey, cuz, I've been trying to reach you," I said before she could start asking questions.

"Ty... are you okay? Where are you?" she asked cautiously.

"Yeah, I'm good. I promise. I've just been trying to keep a low profile because shit has been crazy back here in the states."

"Yeah, I heard. Word was that you got kidnapped by your crazy ass ex who is supposed to be dead," she said.

Inwardly, I groaned because it was obvious that this bitch was missing the subtle hints at normalcy that I was dropping. My eyes flickered up to Roland's, and I could see that he was seconds away from ending the call if I didn't do something fast.

"Bitch, that was just the lie that I let circulate so that I could duck the bullets meant for that nigga, David. You know he was out there in them streets, living a double life or whatever. I had to think about my child first and foremost, you know? Roland saved my life though, and he's right here if you wanna ask him for yourself," I said, flipping the phone on him before turning it back on myself.

"So, you and Roland are... together?"

I didn't know if she was intentionally being dumb or if that was a serious question, but either way, she was pissing me off.

"We're working through our issues for the sake of the baby, but we're still looking over our shoulder because Florida has become a warzone. We need somewhere safe to lay low, and that's why I'm calling. Do you think that you can get us into the country without having to provide passports?" I asked.

"I mean, I'm sure that my baby daddy could make that happen considering that he's the next in line for the throne over here. How soon were you trying to come?"

The smile on this bitch's face made me want to gag, literally, and I finally realized that her sick, twisted ass was enjoying this shit on some level.

"Shaomi, stop playing with me. I just took and told your silly ass that the situation was life and death over here for me and my child."

"Our child," Roland chimed in.

The moment that the expression on her face changed, I knew that she'd heard the ONE THING that I didn't want her to hear, and I knew that shit was about to go all bad.

"Did Roland just say that he's the father and NOT David?" Shaomi asked in a fake whisper.

"That's exactly what he said, and I don't need you running your mouth to the fucking family because it's not their business. The baby's paternity is between me and my baby daddy," I replied testily.

"Oh, I understand, and my lips are sealed like a good pair of legs. Besides, I got my own baby daddy drama going on right now."

If I'd questioned before whether or not this bitch was enjoying this on some level, I knew now that there was no need to question it. She was *absolutely* fucking with me now, and she'd correctly guessed that I hadn't told Roland that David was her baby daddy too. What I didn't understand was to what degree of fuckery Shaomi was willing to play this game.

"Well, bitch, you know that I'm a supportive ear if you need it, so we can talk about whatever is going on between you and your baby daddy when we get there. Will that work?" I asked with exaggerated patience.

"Sure, Ty, but let me talk things over with my baby daddy. I'm expecting him home soon so that I can give him the good news in person."

"Good news? What good news?" I asked, not liking the gut punch I suddenly felt coming.

"Oh, my God, I didn't tell you?! I'm pregnant again... by my baby daddy. We're gonna have a little boy soon," Shaomi replied, grinning broadly.

"Bullshit!" I exclaimed, unable to stop myself.

The smile didn't leave her face, but the camera angle changed, and now, I was looking at her very real baby bump. The next thing that I knew, the phone went dead in my hand.

Chapter 15

(David)

"How big of a team do we need?" Royal asked.

"I don't know, but it has to be enough to hit Bah's secret house in Ft. Lauderdale and attack the port," I replied.

"Well, the port will be an easier job because we just have to hack one of the armed drones that the United States military always keeps roaming the skies. And it shouldn't take more than ten men to do a home invasion, no matter how heavily fortified the house is," he said.

"Do you know someone who can actually hack a military drone?" Carrie asked with a mixture of sarcasm and disbelief.

"I don't need to know someone when I am that someone, sweetheart. If I felt like it, I could park a predator drone on top of your car like the sign for a fast-food restaurant," he replied, giving her a pointed look.

Carrie wisely put her hands up in submission, and Royal turned his attention back to me.

"So, what do you need to make your move?" I asked.

"A laptop for starters."

"I've got one in my truck. Hold on," Carrie said, quickly leaving the room.

The silence that engulfed us was awkward, but I could damn sure live with it if he could.

"I'll work on getting the hired hittas we need," he said, pulling his phone out.

I nodded while retrieving my own phone from my pocket so that I could secretly check on Tesha since I knew that he wasn't looking over her shoulder. My text was short because, at this point, all that we had to discuss was our daughter, so that was what I asked her about. While I was waiting on her to text back, I discovered a message from Shaomi that I'd missed, telling me to call her. I dialed her number and waited on her to answer.

"Hey, baby daddy!" she said, smiling brightly.

"What's up? You and Dayjah good?"

"Yeah, we're good, and Uncle Umar is taking care of us here, but... We miss you," she confessed.

"I know, and I'll be there just as soon as I can eliminate the threat and find Ty. It's almost over so tell my daughter that I love her and miss her."

"What about me? Do you love and miss me too?" she asked seductively.

I already knew what this exact look meant, especially given the tone of her voice and the topic of choice, but now really wasn't the time for the flirtatious shit.

"Let's not play that game, Shaomi, because you already know what it is. I need to focus right now though."

"I'm not playing any game, David. I was actually being serious but whatever," she said, sounding genuinely hurt by my comment.

"Look, I'm sorry. I've just got the weight of the world on my shoulders, and it's a lot. You know how I feel about you."

"Yeah, I do, but I'm worried that your feelings will change once you come back here, and we talk," she said.

"Are you referring to the real nigga radio talk that you mentioned a few days ago? What do you think you could possibly say that would affect the understanding that we have that much?"

Her sudden silence didn't improve the irritation that I was feeling, but I was mindful enough not to take it out on her.

"Just tell me what's going on, Shaomi."

"Okay, look, man, I'm pregnant, and we're having another baby," she blurted out.

"Stop lying."

"Nah, no lies this time and I can send you the pregnancy tests if you want because I took seven of them muthafuckas," she replied.

"But-But you told me that you couldn't get pregnant anymore, Shaomi."

"I know what I told you, nigga, because that's exactly what the doctor told me after I had your daughter. It would seem that he was wrong though because I'm definitely with child, and this ain't no immaculate conception over here," she said seriously.

My mind was spinning, trying to grasp the truth and fit it into what my life looked like in the future, but nothing fit. Another kid? With another woman? Was this a chance at reincarnation for the child I'd just lost, or was this the choke that would shatter the world that I'd built with my wife? I didn't know.

"Say something, David."

At that exact moment, Carrie came back into the room with the laptop, and I had an excuse to end the conversation.

"Listen, I gotta go, but I'll be there soon."

"David, wait..."

I hung the phone up and shut it off before putting it in my pocket.

"You good?" Carrie asked, looking at me closely.

I nodded because I didn't trust my words. I could tell that she wanted to dig deeper and ask more questions, but Royal joined us, and the focus shifted.

"I got the hittas we need, and they're loading up as we speak to head toward Ft. Lauderdale. I don't have an address, but I'm sure that we can find it online," Royal said.

Carrie passed him the laptop, and he immediately perched on the end of the bed to open it and get to work. Carrie stood over his left shoulder, clearly fascinated by his skills, but I didn't mind because that allowed me to make a graceful exit to the bathroom. The first thing that I did was splash water on my face and take several deep breaths to try and regulate my emotions. I understood the birds and the bees intimately, so I knew how this happened, but my mind was still screaming HOW DID THIS HAPPEN?!? Shaomi and I had only had sex once, so the odds of pregnancy should've been infinitely low. And yet, here we were. Arguing the science of it was pointless now, especially when I needed absolute focus. Knowing that I'd handled Shaomi's feelings so poorly weighed too heavily on my mind at the moment for me to focus though, which made me pull my phone back out. I powered it back on with the intention of calling Shaomi, but before I could do that, a video popped up that she'd sent me. When I went to view it, I expected to see her face, but I got the shock of my life because it was Tynesha's face that was front and center. The fact that Shaomi's face was in the top right-hand corner of the video told me that this was a recording of a video call. The time and date told me that it had just occurred within the last hour, and I felt my stomach drop in excitement and anxiety. This was proof that Ty was alive, but Lord only knew what condition she was in. I took a steadying breath before pressing play. The myriad of emotions bouncing through me moved at the speed of light, and the longer the video played, the more unattainable control became. I couldn't believe what I was seeing and hearing, which made me watch the video twice straight through. After that, all I could do was put my phone in my pocket and walk out of the bathroom.

"I hacked into the department of defense and found two drones flying a crisscross pattern between Miami and Cuba. Combined, they easily have enough firepower to knock the port of Miami and the surrounding land off into the water. All you gotta do is say when," Royal said proudly.

"Let's wait until we're in Ft. Lauderdale because with any luck, that'll bring Councilman Bah out of his hiding spot," I said.

Royal nodded and closed the laptop, but Carrie had suddenly zoomed in on me and was moving in my direction.

"Let's load up and move out," I suggested.

"What the hell is going on with you?" Carrie asked in a fierce whisper.

"I'm fine," I replied.

My answer was meant to dissuade her further inquiries, but instead, she stood toe to toe with me and wouldn't let me move past her.

"Royal, can you start taking the weapons to my SUV? It's the blue Ford Explorer parked out front," she said, tossing him the keys.

Never in my wildest dream or nightmares did I think I'd be looking toward Royal to stay and save me, but I did just that. Unfortunately, the nigga was smart enough to take the not-so-subtle hint that Carrie had dropped with her request, and he began taking shit to the truck.

"What is it and don't bother lying to me, David?" she said as soon as the door closed, and we were alone.

There were literally no words formulating in my mind to explain what I'd discovered, so I pulled my phone out and passed it to her.

"The most recent video," I said simply.

She quickly pulled it up and played it out loud. Hearing it all over again caused me to cringe inwardly and close my eyes to ward off what I was seeing in my mind's eye.

"Ohhh, shit," Carrie whispered once the video was done playing.

Royal came back into the room, loaded more guns into the duffle bag he'd made use of, and then he headed back out into the night.

"David, I... I'm so sorry. I can only imagine how you must be feeling right now."

"No, you can't because I really loved her. Yeah, I know that I fuck around sometimes, but it's never taken away from the love that was hers," I said sadly.

"I hear you, and I believe you, but doesn't that mean she could be feeling the same exact way?"

"No, because it's obvious that she's been playing me since the fucking beginning! Everything that she told me about them two was bullshit, and I swallowed it all like any tender dick nigga would!" I raged, feeling fury take over my body.

"David, calm down and think for a second because..."

"Fuck that bitch! I don't wanna talk about it. I just wanna focus on the shit that I can control, and that's who I'm gonna kill next," I stated coldly, snatching my phone out of her grasp.

When Royal came back through the door, I stepped around Carrie and went outside to get some much-needed fresh air. My feet moved by themselves, and I found myself climbing into the passenger seat of Carrie's truck. It was a struggle for me not to pull my phone out and call Shaomi, but I resisted the temptation because I knew that I needed to leave the whole topic alone for the moment. I reached into the center console of the SUV, grabbed everything I needed to roll a blunt, and then I quickly twisted one up. By the time Carrie and Royal made it downstairs, I had smoked half of it, and I was feeling somewhat less tense. I was still homicidal mad though.

"You got the address?" Carrie asked Royal.

"Sending it to the GPS right now."

The LED lights on her dash suddenly came alive, and our destination was spoken out loud by the automated voice.

"We'll be there in an hour, so I want you to hit the port in twenty minutes, and that should give Councilman Bah time enough to get the bad news," I said.

"I got you, and my men should have eyes on the house by then, so we'll know if Bah leaves the house for some reason," Royal replied.

I could feel Carrie looking at me out of the corner of her eye, but I ignored it and kept smoking. Without a word, she started the truck and pulled away from the hotel. We rode in tension filled silence, which I preferred to the counseling mission that I could feel Carrie wanting to engage in. What frustrated me about her was that I expected her to understand on a deeper level because she was married too. There was nothing in my mind that made me believe that Carrie and I fucking meant that she was willing or wanted to leave her husband, nor did it make me question her love for him. Sex was sex, and that was why the shit between Roland and Tynesha hit differently. She'd played with my heart, and sooner than later, she'd learn the consequences for that action.

"That's the house right up there... And those are the hittas," Royal said, leaning forward from the backseat to point.

I observed everything silently as Carrie eased to a stop behind the Chevy Suburban with Royal's people inside. After a few minutes, I got tired of using strategy, choosing instead to trust my instincts.

"Royal, pass me the grenade launcher," I demanded.

Once I had it in my hands, I made sure that it was loaded, and then, I turned to Carrie.

"Stay in the truck and keep it running because we're gonna hit fast and disappear faster."

She nodded and then grabbed me by a fistful of my shirt to pull me toward her. The kiss that she gave me was so quick that I thought I imagined it until she smiled.

"Don't die," she said.

"Not tonight," I replied, opening the door and climbing out.

Royal followed me, and once he signaled, the Suburban emptied its occupants out into the night with us.

"You ready?" Royal asked.

My response was to walk toward the wrought iron gate fence designed to keep intruders out, firing grenades at it. The ground shook mightily as darkness turned to light by fire. I was more than ready. I was motivated.

Chapter 16

(Shaomi)
(Ghana, Africa)
"Mommy, can I go outside with my cousins?"
"Did you finish your breakfast, Dayjah?" I asked, keeping my eyes focused on the computer screen in front of me.
"Yes, Mommy."
"Then you can go out but make sure that you stay with your cousins," I instructed.
The sound of her little feet running echoed around the veranda until she'd disappeared from sight, but my mind was on the future sound my son would make running after his big sister. I secretly always wanted more kids, but I wasn't down with being the stereotypical hood bitch with multiple baby daddies. I had long ago resigned myself to the reality that I wouldn't have more kids simply because I couldn't have David, but all that had changed the day he'd walked into my job. I hadn't known what his intentions were at the time, but my ulterior motive had been in the making from the jump. I knew that it was all about timing because the chemistry between David and I had always been undeniable. All I'd needed was opportunity to come knocking, so when it did, I'd been ready like a runner listening for the starter's pistol. I probably wouldn't have dug so far into my bag of tricks had it not been for Tynesha's traitorous ass, but her presence had made me step my game up. The fact that my own cousin showed no remorse for stealing the love of my life had turned

my heart cold toward her in a way that I never thought possible. Me, Ty, and Tesha had been thicker than thieves, so I would've always expected them to respect the girl code. Ty shattered that illusion, but what I'd discovered later put the icing on the muthafuckin cake and the bitterness on my tongue. Maybe it had been my paranoia, but I preferred to look at it as women's intuition that made me clone David's phone once he'd moved me and our daughter into his apartment. Initially, I'd told myself that I just wanted to know what was happening in case he thought that shielding me from the ugly truth was a good idea. What I didn't expect was to find messages between him, Tesha, and Tonya talking about both of the babies that they were carrying being his biological children. The complete and utter betrayal I'd felt had almost caused me to shoot all of them bitches, family or no family, but something had held me back. At first, I didn't know what it was because it was a distant idea that kept popping up like laughter in the darkness. Then, I slowly started to realize what it was calling to me out of the shadows... It was that wolf named revenge. The concept was simple enough because everyone knew that if you didn't feed your wolves then you were the next thing on the menu. It was by that justification that I gave into the idea of taking back what was rightfully mine and getting pregnant was just the second step. The first move had been to get me and Dayjah to Africa where we could ingratiate ourselves into David's family and his future. The next move from here was to destroy the ties that bound him to my cousins because it was held together by lies anyway. The truth would set us all free, and who better to tell it than the one needing to atone for the lies of the past five years? I saw this as my personal mission, and so I'd played the hand that I was dealt all the way to the point of what I was now masterminding on the laptop in front of me. Having already sent David his video recording of the conversation between me and his wife, I knew that my next move was to send the video to Tesha.

Naturally, there was no need to send the video to Ty, but I wasn't leaving her out because I'd compiled screen shots into a slide show of text messages for Ty to read and enjoy. I was prepared to bring a new definition of 'everything coming to the light that was done in the darkness.' My only regret was that I couldn't be the fly on the wall to witness the destruction left by the wrecking ball I was pushing. It was okay though because I didn't need to see shit go bad to know exactly how this movie was destined to end. Before the credits rolled, I'd be queen of all that I could see from my comfortable position inside David's mansion, and those who'd betrayed me would be buried beneath the hot desert sands. Like Benny the butcher said, everybody couldn't go. There was only room for one queen, and I was the only one qualified for the position available. All hail the queen.

Chapter 17

(Royal)

The moment that we stepped through what was left of the gate, the shooting started, but I was already ready to go guns hot. Just like any fight, it didn't start until the person who initiated contact got hit back, so I was ready for the bullets that were flying my way. Two niggas came running around the corner of the house, but they never made it past the hedges before the rapid fire of my Ruger .45 put them down with big holes in their faces. The darkness came alive with shadows moving and the orange flame of hot bullets bursting from gun barrels.

"Split up!" I yelled, heading toward the back of the house.

I felt the ground move as the picture window at the front of the house exploded from the grenade David fired at it. I didn't know what happened between the hotel and here, but I recognized the madness in his eyes because I'd seen it before in others. He was okay dying here tonight, but I understood how much that could potentially affect the daughter that we now shared. So, that meant I had to protect him from everyone, including himself. When I rounded the corner, I ran into three more armed guards, but the bullets from my men expired their lives before I had the chance to pull my own trigger. Based on the layout of the property that I'd review online, I knew that the house came with a private dock for speed boat access, so it was no surprise to me when

I saw three figures scurrying across the back lawn in that direction.

"Watch my back," I said to my men, taking off at a dead run in pursuit of the three fast moving shadows.

I had no doubt that this was Councilman Bah, Marta, and their son, Paco, so I aimed for the legs of the man on the left and let off three shots. His screams filled the night air as he fell face first into the dew-covered grass, and just as I'd hoped, this brought Marta and Paco to a halt too. Before they could help Bah up, I was standing over top of him with my gun glistening in the moonlight. My initial shots had torn through his calf muscles, but just to be safe, I put two more bullets in his kneecaps, much to his displeasure. When Marta lunged for the gun in my hand, I smacked her across the forehead, opening up a horizontal gash that bled like a cut artery. She fell to one knee and looked up at me with murderous rage in her eyes, but once I turned my gun on Paco, her entire expression changed.

"Please! He's-He's innocent," Marta said in a thick accent that conveyed her Columbian heritage.

"There's no such thing as innocent when you play these games. Didn't you know that?" I asked, smiling sweetly.

"I'll give you whatever you want. Please," Marta begged, crawling to where her son stood and wrapping her arms around his legs.

"What I want is to be somewhere rubbing my lady's feet, but instead, the bitch ass nigga you decided to lay with has forced me to come out and play. This is his fault," I stated.

"I don't-I don't know you," Bah mumbled, grimacing in pain a few feet away.

"You know me though. Don't you, Viktor?" David asked, emerging from the darkness to stand right over top of the councilman.

The look of recognition on Bah's face told me that he understood that the inevitable was coming, and there was nothing he could do about it.

"D-David, be reasonable. You're a businessman, and I'm a businessman, so w-we can work something out," Bah said in a lame attempt to save his life.

"Where's Roland?" David asked.

"I don't- I don't know. I swear. We're hunting for him too, and if you let me live, we will kill him for you. All of this was his fault from the beginning, so it will be our truce through blood," Bah replied.

"Who's next in charge after you?" David asked calmly.

"My nephew, Toot Toot, but he..."

Viktor Bah's explanation was forever silenced by the amount of bullets David dumped into his face without warning. When the clip in his gun was empty, he tucked the gun and reached behind his back for the strap on the grenade launcher with the obvious intent on using that on Bah too.

"David, he's dead," I said, making sure to keep my gun on Paco so that Marta wouldn't try anything stupid.

"I'm just making sure," David replied, dragging his body a few feet away.

Once he reached a safe enough distance from us, he did, in fact, shoot a grenade into Bah's lifeless corpse, causing him to explode in a nighttime shower of blood and guts. Through all of this, I would've expected Paco to be hysterical, or at least crying, but he was doing none of that. His little, black eyes were staring at me so intensely with understanding and hatred that I felt compelled to shoot him, even though he couldn't have been more than eleven years old. Most sane people would argue about how harmless kids were at that age, but I knew exactly who'd I'd been at this kid's age, especially AFTER knowing tragedy in an intimate way. In what was left of my soul, I knew that I was witnessing evil being born, and that left me with only one decision to make.

"Let's get out of here before the cops show up," David said, coming up beside me.

"What about them?" I asked, gesturing toward Paco and Marta.

"Leave 'em. We got who we came for, so now we focus on the nephew if he becomes an issue," David replied.

"That'll be your issue, but this right here, this could be my issue if it's not handled the right way," I explained, holding my gun steady on Paco.

"What are you talking about? He's a kid, and she's just a piece of pussy lucky enough to get pregnant by a nigga with a little power. They're not a threat," David said, dismissing them with a wave of his hand.

His comments made me laugh, but there was no humor in the sound, only understanding.

"You got a lot to learn about the game that you volunteered to play. The rules are simple though. You always play for keeps," I said, shooting Paco in the head and chest.

I turned the gun on his mother and hit her with two shots to her chest as well.

"Let's go," I said to my men, leaving David standing there with a shocked look on his face.

I piled into the Suburban with the hittas and instructed them to make no stops on our way out of town. From Miami, we headed southwest along the Gulf Coast while I arranged for a boat to pick me up from one of the small fishing towns that we were going to pass through. Once I was dropped off and picked up, I was able to rendezvous with my sisters and Tesha aboard the BLUE BLOOD, and only then did I take a deep breath. Of course it was Free that met me when the boat drifted up to the back of my yacht.

"Are you okay?" she asked, scrutinizing me closely in the dark.

"Yeah, I'm fine."

"Royal," Free said, taking my arm to stop me from moving past her.

I didn't avoid her direct eye contact, even though I didn't speak. I'd been around Free long enough to know that I didn't have to speak because she was damn bear clairvoyant when it came to her family. It was one of the traits that I admired and respected about her.

"Whatever happened, you need to remember that ultimately you did what was necessary to protect your family. The role that you've taken in Tesha's and Stormy's lives means that you can't second guess the decisions you make to keep them safe. I know that you used to think that I was just a heartless bitch, and maybe I am, but I don't care because, for my family, I'll be that and so much more. I won't just dance with the devil. I'll teach that nigga some new steps when it comes to me and mines' survival. You're cut from that cloth, little brother, so don't try to hide from it or even try to make it make rational sense to people who don't understand. In this world full of predators, only the apex is safe, but they only remain that way for as long as they can keep their teeth and their claws sharp. Always remember that humans are animals too, only we're higher up on the food chain, which means sometimes we must be demons. That's the ugly truth that will give your family the pretty life they deserve. That's why we do what we do unapologetically."

I absorbed her words of wisdom, allowing them to wash away the ambivalence I'd been feeling since I'd killed Paco. No matter how many times I'd told myself that I'd done what was necessary, it still hit a little different to hear it from someone I knew had done it all. I didn't think that Free took pleasure in killing all the time, but now I understood why her like or dislike didn't stop her gun from going off. Sometimes killing was very much a necessary evil. I gave Free a quick hug before turning and continuing on my way to Tesha's room.

"By the way, since you handled that so swiftly, it will be you who explains all of this to Dad," she called after me.

I threw up my middle finger, which made her laugh, and I kept right on walking. When I got to Tesha's door, I thought about knocking, but instead, I opened the door soundlessly, hoping to glimpse her beauty while she slept.

The first thing that I saw were her eyes in the moonlight, full of unshed tears that made my heart stop dead in my chest. Without a word, she hopped out of bed, and I hurried across the room, catching her in midair as she leapt into my arms.

"Royal," she sobbed, burying her face in my neck.

"I'm here, baby, and it's okay. Everything is okay."

"No, it's not," she replied, leaning back to look up at me.

A feeling of imminent doom came over me, but I gave no outward signs of my anxiousness as I carried her to the bed and sat down with her still in my lap.

"What's wrong, sweetheart? Is Stormy okay?" I asked.

"She's-She's fine, but it's... just look for yourself."

She picked her phone up off the bed and thrust it at me like it was a loaded gun reverse engineered to shoot whoever pulled the trigger.

"What am I looking for?" I asked.

"Look in my text messages and start with the one from Shaomi."

I did as instructed, and I ended up watching a video call between Tynesha and Shaomi. By the end of the video, I better understood the look of utter madness in David's eyes earlier. I had no doubt that he'd seen this video, especially if it had already been sent to Tesha.

"That's crazy... But I need you to explain to me why you're so upset by this because I don't wanna assume to know," I said.

"Read the text that I got from Tynesha and you'll understand."

Again, I followed instructions, and what I read put things into perspective because Ty now knew that David was the biological father of Tesha's and Tonya's babies. There were text messages exchanged between David and Tonya, and David and Tesha, which had somehow found their way to Ty.

The result had been catastrophic because Ty had messaged her own twin, telling her that she was dead to her and vowing that as soon as their babies were born, Tesha would be as dead as their mother already was. This was sibling rivalry on another level, but it was the last part of the text message that disturbed my soul.

"Is she serious?" I asked, looking Tesha in the eyes.

"That's what I'm afraid of. I think my sister is crazy enough to kill my baby, and I don't know what to do."

Chapter 18

(Tynesha)

The tightness in my chest had nothing to do with the stitched-up bullet wound that I was healing from. It was my broken heart causing my breathing troubles, and there was no immediate cure for the pain. It wasn't just that the man I'd trusted with my entire heart had fucked me over so viciously. It was the fact that he'd used my own family to do it. There were so many other women in the world, and yet this nigga had somehow managed to get my sister, my cousin, my mama, AND me pregnant! That had to be some new kind of low down, snake, triple cross type shit. But then knowing that my sister and mom KNEW about each other fucking my man only deepened the fatal wound of David's knife to my heart. I couldn't understand how they could do me like that, how they could be so selfish and so fucking evil that they would actually carry my husband's kids in their wombs. What woman does that? That was the demeaning part that I couldn't get past, but there were no more tears to shed over this. There was only revenge to be plotted.

"You okay?" Roland asked, sitting next to me on the couch.

"That's a dumb ass question."

"No, it's a necessary question. I've known you for a long time, and we've been through a lot of shit, but I've never seen that look in your eyes," he said seriously.

"Oh, yeah, and what look is that? Pain? Fury?"

"No, it's... lost. You look lost, Ty, and I don't know how to help you because this is brand new for me."

When I looked him in the eyes, I could see his genuine concern, which undoubtedly probably surprised me as much as it did him. Since I'd used Roland's phone, I knew that there was no way to hide the truth from him, so I didn't even try. Thankfully, he'd given me a few hours to try and digest as much of this as I could, but some shit I'd never be able to swallow. Some shit was just meant to be regurgitated, especially when you never wanted to forget the taste that it left in your mouth. I knew in my soul that I would hang on to this blood on my tongue until my last breath was drawn, and I was okay with that.

"You really wanna help me, Roland?"

"Of course I do, sweetheart. Despite all that we've been through, I still love you more than anything in the world."

His declaration of love meant nothing to me except for the leverage it provided when it came to the masterclass of manipulation I was in mental preparation for. I would use Roland, without mercy or regard for the consequences for that action, and then I would kill him like David, Shaomi, and Tesha. In the end, I would be the last one alive, but in order for that to happen, I knew that I had to wage war the right way. That meant that my first attack needed to be mental, and thanks to my hoe ass cousin, I had a head start on my dear, sweet David.

"If you really wanna help me, then you must swear to do everything possible to destroy my opps and protect our child. At all costs," I said.

"I swear."

"Nah, don't swear with words. I want you to swear with blood," I demanded.

"What do you mean?"

His question brought a flash of evil genius to mind, which caused me to pull the scalpel from my pocket. When I was sure that William wasn't around, I beckoned Roland to me with one finger wag, and then I whispered in his ear.

"William betrayed you, which means that he betrayed our family, and he can't be trusted. I could've killed you, and it would've been done with his help. Kill him, now, in front of me," I demanded in a sensual whisper.

Roland nodded as he took the scalpel from my hand and concealed it in his own palm. He waited a few seconds, and then, he stood up.

"William, I need you in here for a moment."

Within seconds, we heard footsteps, and then, the good doctor appeared in the living room. I let my eyes drop to half mast, feigning fatigue and giving the impression that I was unaware of what was going on.

"What's wrong, Roland?" William asked.

"I need you to check her stitches because I think she popped some when she moved in her sleep. Take a look," Roland insisted, taking a step back from me.

Without hesitation, William stepped in and leaned over me, which was the biggest mistake of his life. Roland pounced on him, grabbing a fistful of his hair and yanking his head back until his Adam's apple was exposed and visible. William never had time to beg for his life before Roland dragged the scalpel across his throat, spraying me with the doctor's blood that was leaking like a broken sink.

"I'm sorry for getting blood on you," Roland said, tossing the still dying doctor to the floor as he offered me his hand.

"It's okay. It'll come in handy," I replied, pulling myself up off the couch gently and standing.

"What do you mean?"

"Just trust me," I said, leading Roland by the hand to the first bedroom I found on the first floor of the house.

"Take your phone out," I instructed once we were in the room.

While he did that, I looked for the perfect spot in the room to give the angle that I wanted, and once I had it, I held my hand out to him for his phone.

"Take your clothes off and get that dick hard for me," I demanded, taking his phone and setting it to record.

When I had it ready to go, I propped it in between two pillows on the bed, and then, I went to the foot of the bed where I stripped off my clothing. I spent a few minutes fondling my titties as Roland watched from his position next to the bed while he stroked his dick back and forth.

"Come here, Roland," I said in a husky, seductive voice with my eyes locked dead on the phone filming us.

He wasted no time coming to stand behind me, and I immediately felt his dick fucking me in my back.

"Put your dick in me but don't move until I tell you to," I said, still looking at the camera.

I made sure to give an exaggerated sigh of contentment when he penetrated my walls inside me, and then I smiled.

"Now reach around and put your hands on my stomach... then fuck me nice and slow, Daddy," I purred, putting my hands on top of his.

Roland took direction very well, and we spent the better part of an hour making a porno worthy of several awards, even with me being injured. The joy of revenge numbed the pain. We ended the session with him cumming on my face and me rubbing it in with the blood before licking my fingers clean. My smile was dazzling, and that was the image I wanted seared into my husband's mind until death did us part.

Chapter 19

(David)
(Ghana)

"Baby, you need to sleep," Shaomi said softly.

"Don't you think I want to? I just can't make my mind shut off."

"I get it, but this isn't healthy for you, and you know that. They have doctors who can help with your insomnia," she insisted, sitting on my lap in the lounge chair by the pool.

It had become my habit to come out here and think in the solitude of the early morning hours because this was when sleep became the most elusive. This was when the shadows of our bedroom morphed into the fuck fest that I'd witnessed on video between my wife and my sworn enemy. This was when coldblooded murder became my only friend in the world.

"The doctors can't cure what ails me, so there's no point in going to see them. Eventually, I'll get past this. I just have to figure out how."

"I hear you, baby. I really do. Have you reconsidered that distracting yourself may be the best thing for the moment?" she asked.

"Shaomi, I've told you before that I refuse to use you as a distraction, even sexually, because your feelings matter to me too much."

"David, you're not using me, and I hate when you put it that way, like we don't have a past to stand on in this moment. In case you haven't guessed it by now, I'm still very much in love with you, and I will always be. That means that whatever we do is an act of love because I know that you still love me too. You're my Davie Crockett, and I'm your Sha Sha, and no matter what happens in this life or the next, we'll always have each other. Besides our kids, we all we got."

Her words brought some comfort, and they even put a smile on my face, but there was still so much coldness in my heart that I didn't know how to get around it or through it. I just knew that I'd never be over what Ty did to me.

"Bae, I'mma be real with you... This shit has got me fucked up inside, and I ain't never had to deal with no shit like this in my life. It hurts," I confessed.

Shaomi took my face into her hands and looked lovingly into my eyes, and then, she laid a kiss on me that travelled from the depths of her soul. For a moment, all of the emotional turmoil that I felt retreated to a dark corner inside me that I couldn't see, and I took my first deep breath in days. I inhaled everything about this woman in my lap, my first love, into the fiber of my being and let her take the vulnerability that had been the pressure plate on my chest. When she finally lifted her head and smiled, I felt the roots of hope beneath the mud that I was stuck in.

"Crockett, I'm with you, no matter what, no questions asked, no matter how long it takes," she vowed.

"Just because you love me?"

"No, not just because I love you. Also because you deserve my loyalty as much as I do yours. Because I'm your other half like you're mine. And because I know that it's only gonna get darker before we're allowed to come out into the light of our future," she replied.

"I don't know that shit can get any darker for real."

"If you really think that then you're not looking at the chess board through the dimensions of your third eye," she said, giving me a pointed look.

I knew that my confusion had to be evident because I could feel my facial muscles contort, but she said no more and just stared at me with patience that was unnerving.

"Would you just spit it the fuck out?" I said impatiently.

"How do you think this movie ends, David? You think that you're gonna let Roland raise your child, because we both know that there's a good chance that the baby is still yours? And what about Tesha's baby? Have you decided what to do in that situation? No, because you can't see past the pain, and I get that, bae, but that's only temporary. There are decisions that you have to make for the sake of your children, and those decisions don't get easier with time."

I contemplated her words and the implications behind them until slowly the pain gave way to an emotion that suited me better. Fury filled my chest and my heart, helping to clear my vision for the path laid in front of me.

"Tesha won't try to keep me away from my child, but you're right about Tynesha and that bitch ass nigga, Roland. That's a fight that's been made and paid for, but he's got the legal avenues covered again now that he doesn't have to run from Zoe Pound. There's only one thing that I can do... I have to kill that nigga," I concluded.

"No, baby, you're thinking too small. You have to kill both of them because Ty can't be trusted not to poison your own child against you. With her dead, we'll raise the baby as our own with his or her siblings, and that's the way it should be."

What she said made sense, but it was still something that I thought about for a moment, weighing the ramifications of the road that she was suggesting we travel. I never thought that I'd consider murdering the woman that I'd promised forever to, but I remembered the oath that I'd sworn to her in our apartment back in Florida. For all mine, I'll lay yours wasn't exclusive to outsiders. It was for any muthafucka that tried to come for mine because if you weren't family, then you were food for the animals.

"Kill Tynesha?" I asked.

"She has to die, David, and we have to kill her."

"Yeah, you're right... And she'll never see us coming..."

2 be continued...

I'mma Die Bout Mine 4

Lock Down Publications and Ca$h Presents
Assisted Publishing Packages

BASIC PACKAGE $499 Editing Cover Design Formatting	UPGRADED PACKAGE $800 Typing Editing Cover Design Formatting
ADVANCE PACKAGE $1,200 Typing Editing Cover Design Formatting Copyright registration Proofreading Upload book to Amazon	LDP SUPREME PACKAGE $1,500 Typing Editing Cover Design Formatting Copyright registration Proofreading Set up Amazon account Upload book to Amazon Advertise on LDP, Amazon and Facebook Page

***Other services available upon request.
Additional charges may apply

Lock Down Publications
P.O. Box 944
Stockbridge, GA 30281-9998
Phone: 470 303-9761

Submission Guideline

Submit the first three chapters of your completed manuscript to ldpsubmissions@gmail.com. In the subject line add **Your Book's Title**. The manuscript must be in a Word Doc file and sent as an attachment. Document should be in Times New Roman, double spaced, and in size 12 font. Also, provide your synopsis and full contact information. If sending multiple submissions, they must each be in a separate email.

Have a story but no way to send it electronically? You can still submit to LDP/Ca$h Presents. Send in the first three chapters, written or typed, of your completed manuscript to:

LDP: Submissions Dept
P.O. Box 944
Stockbridge, GA 30281-9998

DO NOT send original manuscript. Must be a duplicate.
Provide your synopsis and a cover letter containing your full contact information.

Thanks for considering LDP and Ca$h Presents.

NEW RELEASES

BLOODLINE OF A SAVAGE **BY PRINCE A. TAUHID**

THE MURDER QUEENS 4 **BY MICHAEL GALLON**

THE BUTTERFLY MAFIA **BY FUMIYA PAYNE**

KING KILLA 2 **BY VINCENT "VITTO" HOLLOWAY**

BABY, I'M WINTERTIME COLD 3 **BY MEESHA**

THESE VICIOUS STREETS **BY PRINCE A. TAUHID**

TIL DEATH 2 **BY ARYANNA**

CITY OF SMOKE 2 **BY MOLOTTI**

STEPPERS **BY KING RIO**

THE LANE **BY KEN-KEN SPENCE**

MONEY GAME 2 **BY SMOOVE DOLLA**

THE BLACK DIAMOND CARTEL **BY SAYNOMORE**

CRIME BOSS 2 **BY PLAYA RAY**

THUG OF SPADES **BY COREY ROBINSON**

LOVE IN THE TRENCHES 2 **BY COREY ROBINSON**

TIL DEATH 3 **BY ARYANNA**

THE BIRTH OF A GANGSTER 4 **BY DELMONT PLAYER**

PRODUCT OF THE STREETS **BY DEMOND "MONEY" ANDERSON**

Coming Soon from Lock Down Publications/Ca$h Presents

BLOOD OF A BOSS VI
SHADOWS OF THE GAME II
TRAP BASTARD II
By **Askari**

LOYAL TO THE GAME IV
By **T.J. & Jelissa**

TRUE SAVAGE VIII
MIDNIGHT CARTEL IV
DOPE BOY MAGIC IV
CITY OF KINGZ III
NIGHTMARE ON SILENT AVE II
THE PLUG OF LIL MEXICO II
CLASSIC CITY II
By **Chris Green**

BLAST FOR ME III
A SAVAGE DOPEBOY III
CUTTHROAT MAFIA III
DUFFLE BAG CARTEL VII
HEARTLESS GOON VI
By **Ghost**

A HUSTLER'S DECEIT III
KILL ZONE II
BAE BELONGS TO ME III
TIL DEATH II
By **Aryanna**

KING OF THE TRAP III
By **T.J. Edwards**

GORILLAZ IN THE BAY V
3X KRAZY III
STRAIGHT BEAST MODE III
By **De'Kari**

KINGPIN KILLAZ IV
STREET KINGS III
PAID IN BLOOD III
CARTEL KILLAZ IV
DOPE GODS III
By **Hood Rich**

SINS OF A HUSTLA II
By **ASAD**

YAYO V
BRED IN THE GAME 2
By **S. Allen**

THE STREETS WILL TALK II
By **Yolanda Moore**

SON OF A DOPE FIEND III
HEAVEN GOT A GHETTO III
SKI MASK MONEY III
By **Renta**

LOYALTY AIN'T PROMISED III
By **Keith Williams**

I'M NOTHING WITHOUT HIS LOVE II
SINS OF A THUG II
TO THE THUG I LOVED BEFORE II
IN A HUSTLER I TRUST II
By **Monet Dragun**

QUIET MONEY IV
EXTENDED CLIP III
THUG LIFE IV
By **Trai'Quan**

THE STREETS MADE ME IV
By **Larry D. Wright**

IF YOU CROSS ME ONCE III
ANGEL V
By **Anthony Fields**

THE STREETS WILL NEVER CLOSE IV
By **K'ajji**

HARD AND RUTHLESS III
KILLA KOUNTY IV
By **Khufu**

MONEY GAME III
By **Smoove Dolla**

MURDA WAS THE CASE III
Elijah R. Freeman

AN UNFORESEEN LOVE IV
BABY, I'M WINTERTIME COLD III
By **Meesha**

QUEEN OF THE ZOO III
By **Black Migo**

CONFESSIONS OF A JACKBOY III
By **Nicholas Lock**

JACK BOYS VS DOPE BOYS IV
A GANGSTA'S QUR'AN V
COKE GIRLZ II
COKE BOYS II
LIFE OF A SAVAGE V
CHI'RAQ GANGSTAS V
SOSA GANG III
BRONX SAVAGES II
BODYMORE KINGPINS II
By **Romell Tukes**

KING KILLA II
By **Vincent "Vitto" Holloway**

BETRAYAL OF A THUG III
By **Fre$h**

THE MURDER QUEENS III
By **Michael Gallon**

THE BIRTH OF A GANGSTER III
By **Delmont Player**

TREAL LOVE II
By **Le'Monica Jackson**

FOR THE LOVE OF BLOOD III
By **Jamel Mitchell**

139

RAN OFF ON DA PLUG II
By **Paper Boi Rari**

HOOD CONSIGLIERE III
By **Keese**

PRETTY GIRLS DO NASTY THINGS II
By **Nicole Goosby**

PROTÉGÉ OF A LEGEND III
LOVE IN THE TRENCHES II
By **Corey Robinson**

IT'S JUST ME AND YOU II
By **Ah'Million**

FOREVER GANGSTA III
By **Adrian Dulan**

GORILLAZ IN THE TRENCHES II
By **SayNoMore**

THE COCAINE PRINCESS VIII
By **King Rio**

CRIME BOSS II
By **Playa Ray**

LOYALTY IS EVERYTHING III
By **Molotti**

HERE TODAY GONE TOMORROW II
By **Fly Rock**

REAL G'S MOVE IN SILENCE II
By **Von Diesel**

GRIMEY WAYS IV
By **Ray Vinci**

Available Now

RESTRAINING ORDER I & II
By **CA$H & Coffee**

LOVE KNOWS NO BOUNDARIES I II & III
By **Coffee**

RAISED AS A GOON I, II, III & IV
BRED BY THE SLUMS I, II, III
BLAST FOR ME I & II
ROTTEN TO THE CORE I II III
A BRONX TALE I, II, III
DUFFLE BAG CARTEL I II III IV V VI
HEARTLESS GOON I II III IV V
A SAVAGE DOPEBOY I II
DRUG LORDS I II III
CUTTHROAT MAFIA I II
KING OF THE TRENCHES
By **Ghost**

LAY IT DOWN I & II
LAST OF A DYING BREED I II
BLOOD STAINS OF A SHOTTA I & II III
By **Jamaica**

LOYAL TO THE GAME I II III
LIFE OF SIN I, II III
By **TJ & Jelissa**

IF LOVING HIM IS WRONG…I & II
LOVE ME EVEN WHEN IT HURTS I II III
By **Jelissa**

IMMA DIE BOUT MINE 3 | ARYANNA

BLOODY COMMAS I & II
SKI MASK CARTEL I, II & III
KING OF NEW YORK I II, III IV V
RISE TO POWER I II III
COKE KINGS I II III IV V
BORN HEARTLESS I II III IV
KING OF THE TRAP I II
By **T.J. Edwards**

WHEN THE STREETS CLAP BACK I & II III
THE HEART OF A SAVAGE I II III IV
MONEY MAFIA I II
LOYAL TO THE SOIL I II III
By **Jibril Williams**

A DISTINGUISHED THUG STOLE MY HEART I II &
III
LOVE SHOULDN'T HURT I II III IV
RENEGADE BOYS I II III IV
PAID IN KARMA I II III
SAVAGE STORMS I II III
AN UNFORESEEN LOVE I II III
BABY, I'M WINTERTIME COLD I II
By **Meesha**

A GANGSTER'S CODE I &, II III
A GANGSTER'S SYN I II III
THE SAVAGE LIFE I II III
CHAINED TO THE STREETS I II III
BLOOD ON THE MONEY I II III
A GANGSTA'S PAIN I II III
By **J-Blunt**

PUSH IT TO THE LIMIT
By **Bre' Hayes**

BLOOD OF A BOSS I, II, III, IV, V
SHADOWS OF THE GAME
TRAP BASTARD
By **Askari**

THE STREETS BLEED MURDER I, II & III
THE HEART OF A GANGSTA I II& III
By **Jerry Jackson**

CUM FOR ME I II III IV V VI VII VIII
An **LDP Erotica Collaboration**

BRIDE OF A HUSTLA I II & II
THE FETTI GIRLS I, II& III
CORRUPTED BY A GANGSTA I, II III, IV
BLINDED BY HIS LOVE
THE PRICE YOU PAY FOR LOVE I, II ,III
DOPE GIRL MAGIC I II III
By **Destiny Skai**

WHEN A GOOD GIRL GOES BAD
By **Adrienne**

A GANGSTER'S REVENGE I II III & IV
THE BOSS MAN'S DAUGHTERS I II III IV V
A SAVAGE LOVE I & II
BAE BELONGS TO ME I II
A HUSTLER'S DECEIT I, II, III
WHAT BAD BITCHES DO I, II, III
SOUL OF A MONSTER I II III
KILL ZONE
A DOPE BOY'S QUEEN I II III
TIL DEATH
By **Aryanna**

THE COST OF LOYALTY I II III
By Kweli

A KINGPIN'S AMBITION
A KINGPIN'S AMBITION **II**
I MURDER FOR THE DOUGH
By **Ambitious**

TRUE SAVAGE I II III IV V VI VII
DOPE BOY MAGIC I, II, III
MIDNIGHT CARTEL I II III
CITY OF KINGZ I II
NIGHTMARE ON SILENT AVE
THE PLUG OF LIL MEXICO II
CLASSIC CITY
By **Chris Green**

A DOPEBOY'S PRAYER
By **Eddie "Wolf" Lee**

THE KING CARTEL I, II & III
By **Frank Gresham**

THESE NIGGAS AIN'T LOYAL I, II & III
By **Nikki Tee**

GANGSTA SHYT I II &III
By **CATO**

THE ULTIMATE BETRAYAL
By **Phoenix**

BOSS'N UP I, II & III
By **Royal Nicole**

IMMA DIE BOUT MINE 3 | ARYANNA

I LOVE YOU TO DEATH
By **Destiny J**

I RIDE FOR MY HITTA
I STILL RIDE FOR MY HITTA
By **Misty Holt**

LOVE & CHASIN' PAPER
By **Qay Crockett**

TO DIE IN VAIN
SINS OF A HUSTLA
By **ASAD**

BROOKLYN HUSTLAZ
By **Boogsy Morina**

BROOKLYN ON LOCK I & II
By **Sonovia**

GANGSTA CITY
By **Teddy Duke**

A DRUG KING AND HIS DIAMOND I & II III
A DOPEMAN'S RICHES
HER MAN, MINE'S TOO I, II
CASH MONEY HO'S
THE WIFEY I USED TO BE I II
PRETTY GIRLS DO NASTY THINGS
By Nicole Goosby

LIPSTICK KILLAH I, II, III
CRIME OF PASSION I II & III
FRIEND OR FOE I II III
By **Mimi**

146

TRAPHOUSE KING I II & III
KINGPIN KILLAZ I II III
STREET KINGS I II
PAID IN BLOOD I II
CARTEL KILLAZ I II III
DOPE GODS I II
By **Hood Rich**

STEADY MOBBN' I, II, III
THE STREETS STAINED MY SOUL I II III
By **Marcellus Allen**

WHO SHOT YA I, II, III
SON OF A DOPE FIEND I II
HEAVEN GOT A GHETTO I II
SKI MASK MONEY I II
By **Renta**

GORILLAZ IN THE BAY I II III IV
TEARS OF A GANGSTA I II
3X KRAZY I II
STRAIGHT BEAST MODE I II
By **DE'KARI**

TRIGGADALE I II III
MURDA WAS THE CASE I II
By **Elijah R. Freeman**

THE STREETS ARE CALLING
By **Duquie Wilson**

SLAUGHTER GANG I II III
RUTHLESS HEART I II III
By **Willie Slaughter**

IMMA DIE BOUT MINE 3 | ARYANNA

GOD BLESS THE TRAPPERS I, II, III
THESE SCANDALOUS STREETS I, II, III
FEAR MY GANGSTA I, II, III IV, V
THESE STREETS DON'T LOVE NOBODY I, II
BURY ME A G I, II, III, IV, V
A GANGSTA'S EMPIRE I, II, III, IV
THE DOPEMAN'S BODYGAURD I II
THE REALEST KILLAZ I II III
THE LAST OF THE OGS I II III
By **Tranay Adams**

MARRIED TO A BOSS I II III
By **Destiny Skai & Chris Green**

KINGZ OF THE GAME I II III IV V VI VII
CRIME BOSS
By **Playa Ray**

FUK SHYT
By **Blakk Diamond**

DON'T F#CK WITH MY HEART I II
By **Linnea**

ADDICTED TO THE DRAMA I II III
IN THE ARM OF HIS BOSS II
By **Jamila**

YAYO I II III IV
A SHOOTER'S AMBITION I II
BRED IN THE GAME
By **S. Allen**

LOYALTY AIN'T PROMISED I II
By **Keith Williams**

TRAP GOD I II III
RICH $AVAGE I II III
MONEY IN THE GRAVE I II III
By **Martell Troublesome Bolden**

FOREVER GANGSTA I II
GLOCKS ON SATIN SHEETS I II
By **Adrian Dulan**

TOE TAGZ I II III IV
LEVELS TO THIS SHYT I II
IT'S JUST ME AND YOU
By **Ah'Million**

KINGPIN DREAMS I II III
RAN OFF ON DA PLUG
By **Paper Boi Rari**

CONFESSIONS OF A GANGSTA I II III IV
CONFESSIONS OF A JACKBOY I II
By **Nicholas Lock**

I'M NOTHING WITHOUT HIS LOVE
SINS OF A THUG
TO THE THUG I LOVED BEFORE
A GANGSTA SAVED XMAS
IN A HUSTLER I TRUST
By **Monet Dragun**

QUIET MONEY I II III
THUG LIFE I II III
EXTENDED CLIP I II
A GANGSTA'S PARADISE
By **Trai'Quan**

IMMA DIE BOUT MINE 3 | ARYANNA

CAUGHT UP IN THE LIFE I II III
THE STREETS NEVER LET GO I II III
By **Robert Baptiste**

NEW TO THE GAME I II III
MONEY, MURDER & MEMORIES I II III
By **Malik D. Rice**

CREAM I II III
THE STREETS WILL TALK
By **Yolanda Moore**

LIFE OF A SAVAGE I II III IV
A GANGSTA'S QUR'AN I II III IV
MURDA SEASON I II III
GANGLAND CARTEL I II III
CHI'RAQ GANGSTAS I II III IV
KILLERS ON ELM STREET I II III
JACK BOYZ N DA BRONX I II III
A DOPEBOY'S DREAM I II III
JACK BOYS VS DOPE BOYS I II III
COKE GIRLZ
COKE BOYS
SOSA GANG I II
BRONX SAVAGES
BODYMORE KINGPINS
By **Romell Tukes**

THE STREETS MADE ME I II III
By **Larry D. Wright**

CONCRETE KILLA I II III
VICIOUS LOYALTY I II III
By **Kingpen**

THE ULTIMATE SACRIFICE I, II, III, IV, V, VI
KHADIFI
IF YOU CROSS ME ONCE I II
ANGEL I II III IV
IN THE BLINK OF AN EYE
By **Anthony Fields**

THE LIFE OF A HOOD STAR
By **Ca$h & Rashia Wilson**

THE STREETS WILL NEVER CLOSE I II III
By **K'ajji**

NIGHTMARES OF A HUSTLA I II III
By **King Dream**

HARD AND RUTHLESS I II
MOB TOWN 251
THE BILLIONAIRE BENTLEYS I II III
REAL G'S MOVE IN SILENCE
By **Von Diesel**

GHOST MOB
By **Stilloan Robinson**

MOB TIES I II III IV V VI
SOUL OF A HUSTLER, HEART OF A KILLER I II
GORILLAZ IN THE TRENCHES
By **SayNoMore**

BODYMORE MURDERLAND I II III
THE BIRTH OF A GANGSTER I II
By **Delmont Player**

FOR THE LOVE OF A BOSS
By **C. D. Blue**

KILLA KOUNTY I II III IV
By Khufu

MOBBED UP I II III IV
THE BRICK MAN I II III IV V
THE COCAINE PRINCESS I II III IV V VI VII
By **King Rio**

MONEY GAME I II
By **Smoove Dolla**

A GANGSTA'S KARMA I II III
By **FLAME**

KING OF THE TRENCHES I II III
By **GHOST & TRANAY ADAMS**

QUEEN OF THE ZOO I II
By **Black Migo**

GRIMEY WAYS I II III
By **Ray Vinci**

XMAS WITH AN ATL SHOOTER
By **Ca$h & Destiny Skai**

KING KILLA
By **Vincent "Vitto" Holloway**

BETRAYAL OF A THUG I II
By **Fre$h**

THE MURDER QUEENS I II
By **Michael Gallon**

TREAL LOVE
By **Le'Monica Jackson**

FOR THE LOVE OF BLOOD I II
By **Jamel Mitchell**

HOOD CONSIGLIERE I II
By **Keese**

PROTÉGÉ OF A LEGEND I II
LOVE IN THE TRENCHES
By **Corey Robinson**

BORN IN THE GRAVE I II III
By **Self Made Tay**

MOAN IN MY MOUTH
By **XTASY**

TORN BETWEEN A GANGSTER AND A
GENTLEMAN
By **J-BLUNT & Miss Kim**

LOYALTY IS EVERYTHING I II
By **Molotti**

HERE TODAY GONE TOMORROW
By **Fly Rock**

PILLOW PRINCESS
By **S. Hawkins**

SANCTIFIED AND HORNY
by **XTASY**

THE PLUG OF LIL MEXICO 2
by **CHRIS GREEN**

THE BLACK DIAMOND CARTEL
by **SAYNOMORE**

THE BIRTH OF A GANGSTER 3
by **DELMONT PLAYER**

BOOKS BY LDP'S CEO, CA$H

TRUST IN NO MAN
TRUST IN NO MAN 2
TRUST IN NO MAN 3
BONDED BY BLOOD
SHORTY GOT A THUG
THUGS CRY
THUGS CRY 2
THUGS CRY 3
TRUST NO BITCH
TRUST NO BITCH 2
TRUST NO BITCH 3
TIL MY CASKET DROPS
RESTRAINING ORDER
RESTRAINING ORDER 2
IN LOVE WITH A CONVICT
LIFE OF A HOOD STAR
XMAS WITH AN ATL SHOOTER